SHINY THINGS

BOOK 1 GRETEL KOCH JEWEL THIEF

SAMANTHA PRICE

IN THE SILENCE of the dark mansion, Gretel Koch slowly approached the safe. Once she reached it, she lowered herself to her knees and flicked on the flashlight strapped to her forehead.

She studied the flat base inside and saw the screws she knew would be there. This safe had a secret compartment and if the robbers from the night before had missed it, she'd be the owner of some iconic and rare jewels. If she was wrong, she'd just risked everything for nothing.

Gretel reached into her knapsack and pulled out the automatic screwdriver and undid the single screw in each corner. Then with a bent nail, she pulled on the base and it moved.

Second obstacle overcome.

The first one had been getting into the house, but

tonight that was made easier by knowing the owner wasn't due back until the next day.

When the base of the safe was removed, she turned her attention to what was hidden. She couldn't believe what she saw by her flashlight.

It was empty.

Completely.

Nothing.

It made no sense. Why have a secret compartment in the safe if they didn't use it? The police had never mentioned the secret compartment so she knew they didn't know it was there.

That only meant one thing. The jewels had been taken out before Mr. Welch had been killed. His murder was an inside job. Welch wasn't shot while disturbing intruders. He'd been murdered and the robbery staged.

Lights outside distracted her. Immediately, she flicked off her flashlight and ran to the window to see a car. When the car door opened, she saw Mrs. Welch home, ahead of schedule. Then a man got out of the car and followed her to the house.

Gretel watched in the darkness. Surely the woman wouldn't cross the tape. Surely she would turn around and stay in a hotel for the night. The police would've told her the situation. When Gretel heard the door open and muffled voices coming from downstairs, she was shocked.

Suddenly the house lit up like a beacon, inside and out.

There was no time to waste.

She had to leave. As quietly as she could, she closed the heavy door and after she spun the dial, she noticed the shelf and the screws.

This wasn't like her. She was panicking.

Calm down.

She placed the shelf along with the screws between the wall and the safe, out of sight. Then she raced to one of the bedrooms that lined the back of the house intending to climb out the window and make her way down the sandstone blocks that made up the facade of the house.

The first door she tried was locked. Moving onto the next one, it too was locked. There was no time to pick a lock. She couldn't believe her misfortune when she found the third and last bedroom on that side of the house was locked too.

Then she remembered the servants' stairway that led to the kitchen. She raced to the corner and ran carefully down the narrow stairs.

When she arrived in the kitchen, she heard footsteps. She froze. Would she make it to the back door without being seen? There wasn't enough time.

She spied a butler's pantry adjoining the kitchen and slipped into it, closing the door behind her.

"Check the house," she heard Mrs. Welch command. "Every inch of it."

"I'm on it. You wait right here," the man replied, his voice distinctively raspy-sounding.

How did Mrs. Welch know someone was in the house? Gretel realized that it was the security system. She'd had it disarmed. Mrs. Welch would've seen the light off. Systems like the Welches' weren't overly complicated despite what treasures they had. It was surprising they hadn't been hit earlier, if indeed this last one had been a genuine hit.

Gretel closed her eyes tightly. *Leave. Please leave.*

Where was that nightly patrol car? It was bad timing since the car had just done its drive past. It was supposed to be driving past the house at regular intervals, but that meant it wouldn't be back for ages. Even Mrs. Welch wasn't allowed back in her home yet.

Lowering herself to the floor, the bitter regret of coming back to the house stung through her body. She'd been wrong. No crime was perfect. The risk of being caught was always a lingering threat looming overhead like an angry cloud.

With her sleeve, she wiped the sweat that dripped from her forehead.

In her mind, she'd had nothing to lose and everything to gain by coming back here tonight. She'd been too sure of herself. It had promised to be so easy when she'd played it out in her mind. Why hadn't she resisted the temptation?

If she was sent back to prison, it'd be as good as a death sentence since she'd double-crossed those girls to suit her own ends. The haunting images of all the prison inmates flashed through her mind.

When she heard footsteps on the stone kitchen floor, she knew it was the end. Would she be killed in this house, and die here just like Glen Welch? She backed further into the corner, but there was no place to hide. Feeling her heartbeats throbbing inside her head, she drew a large knife out of the rack, ready to defend herself.

She'd never liked violence, but self-defense was an entirely different matter.

The Previous Day

GRETEL AWOKE in her upper east side New York City apartment, thankful to be in her own bed. She was still conscious that she had to be useful to the FBI or she'd find herself back in prison. As yet they had given her no concrete guarantees that they wouldn't proceed with the charges that had been mounting against her. For now, she was free and one day at a time was how she had to play it.

She took time to leisurely stretch her hands above her head. Freedom had never felt so good. Only a couple of weeks ago she had been facing the prospect of twenty-five-to-life. Somehow, life always had a way of surprising her to the extremes.

She pulled the covers up around her neck, thinking about Ryan Castle, the man who had double-crossed her and brought her to the attention of the FBI, and who was the direct cause of her getting arrested. Ryan had stolen her latest heist of diamonds and stashed them somewhere. Then he gave evidence against her telling them she'd hidden the jewels. And then, most annoying to her, they'd dropped the charges against him in exchange for his testimony.

Even though she had made a deal with the FBI, she still wasn't sure exactly what they expected of her. Sooner or later she'd find out but, for now, all she could focus on was getting those diamonds back.

"One thing at a time," she said aloud as she flung back the covers and bounced out of bed. She was halfway to her en suite bathroom when she turned back and picked up her cell phone and dialed the hospital where Ryan was recovering from a gunshot wound.

"Hello, could you tell me the ward and room number of Ryan Castle? I'm his sister," she lied. "He was in Emergency but now I believe he's in a private room."

"Yes, Ryan Castle. I can confirm we have a patient by that name, but regulations don't allow me to release any further information by phone."

"Thank you." She ended the call. At least she knew he was there. She'd be able to learn more once she reached the hospital. A little chat with Ryan while he lay there feeling sorry for himself might point her to where the diamonds were stashed. For certain he'd have a guard on his door, but she'd find her way around that when she got there. Circumstances always worked in her favor.

After she took her time showering, she changed into some casual clothes—jeans and a soft pink blouse with a barely visible vine pattern. Then she blow-dried her dark hair to give it extra bounce. A luxury that had been denied her in prison.

Time for makeup. She examined her skin under the strong daylight. It had suffered from the short prison stay, with the poor diet and the lack of good skin products. A facial and a salon peel would help get it back to normal. There were so many things she needed to do, but they'd have to wait until she got the diamonds. She sorted through her array of makeup and found her heaviest foundation. After she'd sponged it over every inch of her face and jawline, she applied the liquid black eyeliner. She gave it a cat-like kick up at the sides to accentuate her deep blue eyes. She finished off with a dash of neutral lip color and a dash of Desert Peach blush.

Taking two paces back, she stared at her reflection in the bathroom mirror. Thank goodness she looked nothing like her mug shot that had been on the front page of every newspaper in the country, and across much of the world.

People would forget in time, she hoped.

She headed into her walk-in-closet and hesitated at her jewelry box. Given the recent attention she was attracting, she decided against wearing her usual diamonds, and she had no costume jewelry. For her, it was either the real thing or nothing. Moving on to her shoes, she pushed her feet into her favorite platforms. They were high yet comfortable.

It was a bright day, the sun was shining, the traffic from the street five floors down was rumbling. Since she was keen to leave for the hospital, there was no time for breakfast, but she needed coffee. She flipped on the coffee machine and downed a quick espresso, set her cup in the sink, grabbed her handbag and opened the door.

In front of her, his hand raised to knock, stood Jack Fletcher.

He stared at her. "Going somewhere?"

CHAPTER 2

GRETEL KOCH LOOKED up at the handsome FBI agent as she tried to steady her breathing. Even though she was tall in heels, this man still towered over her. "I'm just headed out to have a decent breakfast."

"It'll have to wait." He pushed past her into her apartment.

"Come in," she said, turning to follow and closing the door behind her with her foot. "Thanks, don't mind if I do," she said a little sarcastically on his behalf, as if he'd properly finished the social niceties.

When he was in the center of the room, he spun around to face her. "Coffee?"

"I've just had one, thanks for asking."

He grinned showing his perfect white teeth. "I meant, would you make me one?"

"Oh. Sure."

Tilting his face up, he wrinkled his nose and sniffed the air. "I can smell Arabica beans with a touch of vanilla."

"That's right. It's my favorite blend." She put her bag on the couch and headed to the kitchen area of her open-plan apartment.

"I do know my coffee." He came closer and sat on one of the four stools that were pushed against the counter. His hand ran over the marble. "Nice marble."

"Calacatta."

"Hmm. And who said crime doesn't pay?"

A chill ran through her body.

Was Jack trying to trick her into saying something—trying to get information from her?

She'd never been on trial for her crimes and she'd never officially confessed to any of them. They'd offered her a deal in exchange for dropping all charges. Seeing she'd been denied bail, it was either accept their offer or rot in jail for ... oh, two or so years awaiting a trial.

Even though she and Jack were supposedly on the same side, she couldn't drop her guard with him. As she opened her mouth to make some excuse for her extravagant apartment—the same one she gave the IRS —he spoke again.

"I've got a job for you," he told her. "Now's your chance to help us."

"And what's that?"

"We have something that's come up and it's right up your alley."

It was rotten timing. Just when she was looking forward to getting the truth out of Ryan, trapped in his hospital bed with nowhere to run and totally at her mercy. "Can it wait? Say, until tomorrow? There are some urgent things I need to—"

"No. It's a murder."

Why was that 'right up her alley?' It wasn't as though she'd ever killed anyone or been involved in anything like that. In fact, she didn't like violence of any kind. Her nose crinkled. "Murder?"

"Yes. A murder associated with a robbery."

"I don't know how I'd be able to help you. I was never involved in anything like that." She handed him a cup of black coffee. "I'm sorry. I don't have milk, or sugar."

"That's okay. I prefer it black with no sugar anyway." He took a sip, raising an eyebrow in appreciation. "The first days after a murder are the most crucial. That's why we need to make a move now. When I was called in on it, I knew it was perfect for you. It'll be a good one for you to cut your teeth on." He took a mouthful of coffee.

She leaned forward on the counter across from him. "I didn't know you'd be needing my services so soon. You really haven't even told me what's expected of me. Not in detail anyway."

"We believe your input from the criminal perspective will be valuable."

Criminal? She never saw herself as a criminal. It

bugged her the way he thought she was one.

Jack was getting in the way of her plans, but she didn't see a way around it. "Okay. Let's go." The sooner she got it over with, the sooner she could get the truth out of Ryan. If luck was on her side, and it normally was, she'd be holding the diamonds in her hands tonight.

He drained the last of his coffee and then walked over and placed the cup in the sink beside hers. "It's all right to leave it here?"

"That's fine. I'll take care of them later. Thanks."

He looked round about him. "Nice apartment you've got here."

Again with the apartment-talk. This wasn't good. She'd bought the apartment years ago and had paid millions for it back then. If they took that from her, as proceeds of crime, she didn't know what she'd do. It was the only place she'd ever truly felt at home. "Thanks. It's okay."

"The views are incredible."

"I think so. Shall we go?" She grabbed her bag and then held the door open for him. He walked through.

When they were heading down in the elevator, his cell phone beeped. He pulled it out of his pocket. "Jack Fletcher." Then he hesitated and looked at her. She knew it was something about her. Had they changed their minds? Gone back on their deal? Gretel hated not being in control. That was the reason she worked alone wherever possible.

He ended the call. "Ryan Castle has disappeared from the hospital. Do you know anything about that?"

CHAPTER 3

Her mouth opened in shock; she'd only just called the hospital. "He's gone? How's that possible?"

"I'm not sure. I've just been informed."

"He's going after those diamonds. Is that where we're going, to find the diamonds?"

"No." He drew his eyebrows together and stared at her as the elevator doors opened. He put his hand across the doors to keep them open, and she stepped out. When he caught up to her, he pulled her to one side of the foyer. "I just told you we're investigating a murder with a robbery."

Frustration whirled through her head. With Ryan gone, how was she going to get anything back from him? Now she wasn't captive in prison, she was Jack's personal captive. That was what it felt like. She rubbed her head. She had to pull it together or Jack would think she wasn't any use to them. "I'm sorry. This has come as a shock. I mean, why would he leave the hospital? He was shot and he was in the intensive care unit."

When people entered the building, Jack whispered to her, "We'll talk in the car."

He ushered her out of the foyer, and they walked two blocks to his car while he made a call from his cell phone. When they reached his car, he opened the passenger door for her.

She slid into the seat and buckled her seatbelt.

Once they were on the move, he said, "I want you to put your feelings for your boyfriend out of your mind. He's our problem now. You're best to forget about him. We're already working on locating him. He won't get far."

Was he kidding? He thought she was still in love with Ryan. What a joke. Especially when Ryan had given up all he knew about her and was prepared to testify against her. "Find him and you'll find those diamonds."

"Maybe." He gave her a sidelong glance and she knew that he wasn't fully convinced Ryan had the diamonds.

"Look, I know you think I have the diamonds, but I've been telling you the truth all along. He left me to drown in that car after he grabbed them. I even saw him running along the shoreline with the bag that the diamonds were in."

"When we caught up with him, there were no

diamonds and no bag. He swore himself black and blue you had hidden the diamonds. He said they were never in the car. We had the car brought up and we sent divers down and there was nothing about."

"He's obviously lying. You didn't need to send divers anywhere. He stashed the diamonds by the riverbank and since then he would've gone back to get them." That's what she would've done.

"Possibly. I'll need to trust you about that."

"Yes, good. Trust me, because I'm telling the truth. I mean, you must believe me, otherwise you wouldn't have offered me the deal." She quickly added, "Which I accepted."

"We'll see."

"Speaking of the deal, when will it become official? Will there be some kind of paperwork?"

She saw him nearly grimace and his fingers gripped the steering wheel tighter. "It's underway. It's not going to be that easy. We've got other countries involved and they want justice. The fact that you're now helping us isn't going to appease them."

"There's no proof I did anything. They're all jumping on the bandwagon."

He took his eyes off the road for a moment and stared at her. "You and I know exactly what you've done."

Did he know everything? Something told her he did. She didn't see why she was working with him, helping him, when she had nothing in writing. Still, it was her only hope at this point. She turned her head and looked out the window. "Where are we going?"

"A man by the name of Glen Welch was found murdered. He was found in his study in front of an empty safe. The safe had been full of jewelry. We don't have an exact estimate but it's in the millions."

"And you think I know something about it?"

"Don't worry, we don't think you had any involvement."

"Well, that's a good start. Where are we going?"

"The Hamptons."

"That's quite a distance away from your jurisdiction, isn't it?"

"I don't have a jurisdiction. You could say it's all over the country. State-to-state." He drove to a drive-through hamburger place. "How does a burger sound for breakfast?"

"Yes, please." How would she find Ryan now? He'd be long gone by the time she got back to the city.

He ordered burgers and more coffee for both of them before they drove on. Then he told her all that he knew about the case.

"And why did they call you in?"

"The value of the jewelry that was stolen, mainly. It's attracting a lot of media attention. They've had three helicopters flying over this morning already. We've had to turn five news channels away. It's a high-profile case with high profile people. Glen Welch was one of the city's best-known lawyers."

"His name is familiar."

"We've got a long drive." Jack turned the music on, drowning out any possible conversation.

Gretel spent her time emailing her sister and some friends from her phone, so the time in the car wouldn't be a complete waste.

"It's just up here at the end."

Gretel saw news vans lining the street and one cameraman was out of the car filming the Welch house from the street. As they got closer, Gretel slid down in the seat until they drove past them through the large gates flanked by two uniformed policemen.

As they drove up the long driveway, Gretel admired the gardens and the perfectly trimmed hedges that divided them. "The gardens are breathtaking. They must have at least one full-time groundskeeper."

"The upkeep must be horrendous." He parked in the circular driveway in front of the house in between two white vans and four police cars.

As men in white evidence-collection suits came out of the house, Gretel stared up at the white mansion. "I know this place. I came here as a kid a few times. Who did you say died?"

"Glen Welch. Josephine, his wife, first owned it with her original husband, Earl Butterworth."

"Oh, so the victim, Glen, was her second husband?"

"Correct."

She stared at the grand double doors and the wide stairs that led up to them. It was the kind of place that

SAMANTHA PRICE

would have servants. "I can see why she wouldn't want to leave. It's stunning, but I wouldn't like the job of looking after it. I think I used to come here for events when I was a child. Whoever lived here donated heavily to my father's ministry. It must've been Butterworth, the first husband, who did."

"Your father, the famous evangelist? Interesting connection."

"He's not famous. He's just on TV sometimes. That's right, Glen Welch. That's why that name sounded familiar. He's the one who bought up all the iconic movie star jewelry." Someone putting yellow and black crime scene tape around the building distracted her. "So, he was shot you said?"

"Yes. They've taken the body, but everything else remains. It's a wonder these people weren't a target of yours."

She shook her head. He was right, she was considering it at one point, but then was distracted by bigger fish overseas. "Yes, they had pieces worthy of stealing, but I'd never steal someone's private collection." She looked up at the house. "And not from their home."

"A thief with a conscience."

It was refreshing that he believed her lies. "I like to call them standards. A personal code of ethics, if you will. Talking about ethics, what's happening with Ryan Castle? Shouldn't you be looking for him?" Her stomach churned. She felt like an athlete ready to run a race, and Jack was holding her back.

20

"I've got people on it. Relax. Trust me. Today, we're focusing on this." He stared at her until she nodded in agreement. "Josephine Welch was on holiday in Bermuda with her adult daughter from her first marriage."

"Yes, that would be Gizelle. I know her. She's a friend of one of my sisters." Gretel made a face.

"You knew Gizelle and didn't make the connection regarding her stepfather just now?"

"No. It took me a while. I've had a lot on my mind. Gizelle and I have never gotten along."

"No love lost there, eh?"

"She's not a very nice person. My sister and she have been friends for years. I'm not sure why."

"Mrs. Welch's lawyer has given us a list of all that was stolen from the safe. They took everything, apart from Mrs. Welch's engagement ring and whatever else she had with her at the time."

"I'll soon know if they were professionals. Not too professional to have been detected when they were in the middle of the job."

"We don't know for sure yet if he surprised the robbers or whether something else played out." They walked toward the front door, and he said, "Now are you getting the idea why we need your criminal mind on the case? Your lack of empathy for the family of the man who was killed enables you to focus on the crime at hand." He motioned her to move forward to the house.

He had her all wrong. Just because she liked to take things that didn't mean she was heartless. "Hey, I take offense to that. I'm a reformed woman. I did say it was too bad about him getting killed even though I didn't know him at all."

He raised his eyebrows as though she was doing little to convince him.

As she walked up the front steps, she added, "I was a kid last time I was here and it was most likely husband number one living here back then."

As they walked to the house, he whispered, "Don't talk to anyone and if anyone asks, you're my assistant."

CHAPTER 4

THE EVIDENCE TECHNICIANS had left by the time they reached the upstairs study where the murder had taken place. As Gretel walked into the room behind Jack, she saw the white chalk marks on the floor just like in the movies. The stench of death and the peculiar smell of old books filled her nostrils. She looked around at the wall of antique leather-bound books. Death and musty paper weren't a pleasant combination.

Any other time she would've looked through the old books, but the safe in the corner drew her attention.

"You can touch things as long as you don't move them," Jack said.

When she was in front of the safe she saw it was a Morton 800. Made by Morris Morton in the eighties. She knew her safes. It was certainly sturdy and worked well enough in a non-commercial setting. It wasn't known by many that some of this model were made with hidden sections. The internal base unscrewed. Gretel had to wonder if it was one of those. A closer inspection would reveal the answer.

She turned around to see Jack crouched down examining the patterns on the blood-stained carpet, so she turned back to get a better look at the base of the safe. Yes, there was a separate section for the base. It appeared undisturbed. If they'd killed someone, they wouldn't hang around to screw the base back down, not so perfectly anyway.

Now she was torn. If she told Jack about this, it could help with the investigation, but what if there were delightful untouched treasures hidden there? Treasures that perhaps no one would miss especially since they thought everything was taken.

The family was obviously insured and who would look in her direction for jewelry that had already been stolen? With Mrs. Welch due back tomorrow what was stopping her coming back under the cover of darkness?

It was like free candy waiting to be eaten, and the fact that the house would be empty tonight was way more than a temptation.

It was a gift.

She would've thought twice about it had the FBI given her official paperwork about her pardon, but what assurances did she have of her freedom at this point? Jack kept telling her to trust him, but she'd trusted one man before and where had that gotten her?

"Why are you staring at an empty safe?"

She faced Jack. "I wasn't even seeing it. I was zoned out, thinking about all the pieces they bought over the years. They certainly had a lot. Jewelry once owned by European royalty and some pieces that Elizabeth Taylor once owned. I remember one diamond they bought from India, nearly as big as an egg." She looked back at the safe. Surely the best pieces would be in the hidden section.

"I have the list of everything that was taken. Mrs. Welch's lawyer was good enough to fax it to us."

"Yes, you said that. She must be dreadfully upset. They had pieces that can never be replaced." Gretel walked to the other side of the room, still not sure why she was there or what she was supposed to conclude. She walked back to Jack. "You say Josephine, the wife, is coming back tomorrow?"

"Yes."

"Does Gizelle live here too?"

"No. Only Mrs. Welch, and the servants."

"And, where are the servants?"

"Mrs. Welch gave them the week off since she was going away. Her husband was happy to be on his own and look after himself. I believe the cleaning staff was given the week off as well. She often holidayed without him and he preferred to keep working."

"What lawyer sent in the list of stolen items?"

"I can't say off the top of my head. Glen Welch was a lawyer too. Did I mention that?"

"You might have. Interesting that another lawyer had a list of what was in the safe to send you. What an organized woman Mrs. Welch is."

"I don't know the name, but I know he was Mr. Welch's business partner. People with this type of wealth are normally very well organized. She would've had them itemized with the insurance company as well."

No longer being able to take the pressure, she stared at him with her hands on her hips. "What am I supposed to tell you?"

"Your thoughts, just like you've been doing just now."

"Well, I don't understand this; why would they do it when he was home? Why not when he was at work?"

"That's also the very thing that has me puzzled. They might've needed him to give them the combination. There was no sign of a struggle but perhaps they had a gun pointed at him the whole time."

If that was right, that meant Mr. Welch wouldn't have told them about the hidden section. If the Welches were smart, they would've had professional replicas made which they kept in the top section of the safe. That was her best scenario. She was getting more excited by the minute. "That is awful if that's what happened."

"Unless they took a risk and did it at night hoping he'd be asleep. Access was gained through the conservatory door." When they got to a window he pointed at a smaller house. "That's where the servants live. A manservant and a maid, married to each other."

"Ah. Convenient. Maybe they had to break in when Mr. Welch was home because the security system would be turned off. Maybe they got someone to give him sleeping tablets, but they didn't work, and he interrupted them."

"We'll have to wait to see what the autopsy tells us and see what fingerprints the team has been able to lift. They have also taken all the food and alcohol out of the house for testing."

"Good move. Very thorough."

"Thank you. Feel free to keep having a look around, but I'll have to follow you."

"Don't worry, I'm not going to slip any silverware into my pocket."

He smiled at her. "All the same…"

"Tell me about the security system and their security measures."

As they walked, he talked, not knowing there was anything left in the house to steal.

Now Gretel was focused on what might be hidden in the safe. With this new opportunity, she was no longer so concerned about Ryan Castle and his disappearance from the hospital.

CHAPTER 5

As soon as she got back to her apartment, she opened one of her disposable cell phones and lay down on her couch, propping her feet up on cushions.

"Kent, it's me."

"Hi there."

She gave him the address of the Welch mansion. "Have a look at the security system. I've been there today and I'm going back there tonight. Also, Jack Fletcher, my new boss tells me Ryan Castle has vanished from the hospital. He's on the move—find him."

"You sure about this?"

Kent rarely questioned her about anything. "Sure about which part?"

"You're going back there for what exactly?"

She blew out a deep breath. She'd told him the previous day she was going straight, helping the FBI.

"It's the perfect crime, Kent. I can't pass it up." She filled him in about the murder, the absent wife and staff, and the hidden section in the safe. "You see, they won't think I've stolen something if they're convinced it's already been stolen by someone else." When he was silent, she asked, "Well, would they?"

"I guess not. Hey, do whatever you want. Keeps me in a job." She heard the keys on his computer clicking. He then gave her information on the security system at the Welch house.

"Perfect. That's what I figured."

"What do you need me to do?"

"Disable the security system, without it going to back-up power."

"While also making it look like everything's working perfectly."

"Exactly," Gretel agreed. "If you can."

"Ouch! What do you mean, 'If I can?' Of course I can. You need a driver?"

"No. I'll be in and out of there with no problem at all. I don't need you for this."

"All the same, perhaps I should come with you?"

"No." She didn't want to complicate something that was going to be simple. Kent's time was better served finding Ryan.

"Don't take any risks and good luck. I'll have it disabled between eight and eleven."

"That's perfect."

"Please have a phone on you and I'll be on standby all night just in case. Call me when it's done."

"Sure. Don't worry. This will be easy breezy."

"Haven't you always said never to be over confident?"

"I know, and that's true. I'm not over confident. I just have a positive attitude about it."

"Okay. Be sure to call me when you're finished so I don't stay awake all night worrying."

"Will do."

IT WOULD'VE BEEN foolish to take her own car. She needed a rental car for the job and for that, she needed one of her fake IDs. A driver's license should do the trick. She went to her study and pulled out a fake one from a secret compartment in her desk. Then she emailed Kent, gave him the fake name and got him to book her a rental car. He'd email her the details.

When she'd been arrested, her apartment had been searched but they hadn't found any of her goodies that she'd cleverly hidden throughout. She headed to the couch, flipped open her laptop computer and got into the dark web so her searches couldn't be traced, and typed in the Welches' home address. Up came a map and after she'd studied it in relation to the streets and the houses nearby, she chose a point of entry—through the conservatory. The same way as the people who did the first robbery. That meant she'd have to scale that large fence she'd seen at the back of the property, entering and exiting through a neighbor's backyard. She just hoped the neighbors didn't have a vicious dog.

Her email beeped. She clicked it open. Kent had booked the car.

She slipped into black stretchy pants and a T-shirt and pulled on joggers. She swept her hair up into a ponytail, hoping that if anyone saw her, they'd think she was going to the gym. She took out a large bag and placed her tools of the trade inside it—her headband flashlight, knife kit, and implements to open locks—all rolled up in a towel to add to the gym illusion, along with two pairs of gloves tucked alongside and out of sight. Lastly, an untraceable and disposable phone for emergencies, and a black hooded pullover.

She then left her main cell phone at home, slipped out of the apartment and changed taxis enough times to ensure she wasn't followed before she arrived at the place Kent had booked the rental car.

Just as the sky was turning from dark blue to black, she arrived at the street where she'd planned to park. Now she had to wait until eight. Looking up at the stars in the sky, she wondered what her life would be like now if she'd never met Ryan Castle. She'd been about to retire knowing that the odds were against her continuing her career undetected. It was only a matter of time. Why had she been so quick to tell him what she did?

She rested her head back and closed her eyes. He'd told her many things about himself and the crimes he'd committed, and the people he'd tricked out of their fortunes. They were people who deserved it, he'd said. People involved with human trafficking and cruelty to animals. He'd brought them down, or so he'd said. Now she didn't know if anything he'd told her was true. Still, it had made her open up to him. He'd convinced her to do one last job. Rather than work with Kent and her people, she'd trusted him. It had been dumb and it'd cost her freedom.

Don't fix what isn't broken. She should never have changed her formula that had worked so well.

"Stop thinking about him," she said aloud. A glance at the clock in the car told her there was still half an hour to wait, but she wasn't nervous—not for this small job. Earlier that day, she'd noted the layout of the whole house, as well as exit and entry points.

Her thoughts drifted to Jack Fletcher. Would he or could he be interested in a woman like her? She could see herself with a man like Jack, honest, dependable. Someone who only saw the good in her. From the way he acted he seemed to think she was reformed. If she was married to a man like him, that would give her the best incentive to change her ways forever. A house in the suburbs, maybe a couple of kids and a dog. Yes, definitely a dog.

But that imaginary life wouldn't be all sunshine and lollipops, she realized. Her days would be filled with boring mundane things and the highlight would be going to the gym or getting her hair done. She winced at the thought of laundry and having to dream up different dinners to cook each night, as well as the chore of driving kids to soccer on the weekend. Soccer was something she never understood. Being a housewife and mother was for other people, she realized the more she thought about it.

Looking out the window at all the grand houses owned and lived in by normal, yet affluent people, she had to wonder why she couldn't be satisfied with normal.

Gretel drummed her fingertips on the steering wheel. Nearly eight. She'd wait for a few minutes after the hour to be sure the alarm was off.

At five after eight, Gretel made her move.

CHAPTER 6

SHE PULLED on her hooded pullover, got out of the car and slung her knapsack over her back. Then she jogged steadily to look as though she were exercising if anyone saw her. Two streets over and then she located the house that backed onto the Welch mansion. There were no vicious dogs and they had no fence except at the back of their property. It was an easy climb and when she got to the top, she climbed down the hedge branches. Then by the light of the moon, she sprinted to the house making sure her hood covered her face. She reached the conservatory and made her way through to the backdoor. The house was in darkness.

"Like taking candy from a baby," she murmured to herself as she took out her lock picking tools. "Who gives a baby candy? It wouldn't be so easy taking it from a toddler, though." With the help of the two metal implements, she picked the lock. The click of a lock opening always put a smile on her face.

Then she pulled on her gloves and wiped the entire lock area with her sleeve. After she moved through the door, she closed it behind her. With the alarm off, the only thing to worry about was the patrol car she'd been told would be driving by every so often.

There was no fancy fingerprint-coded entry for this house. The security was surprisingly undercooked for the treasures they'd had within. "No wonder they were robbed. It's amazing it hadn't happened sooner."

Mrs. Welch wasn't due until tomorrow and could only come back into the house once the crime tape was removed.

Gretel moved farther in and closed the door behind her. In the darkness, she found her way. It was hard not to turn on a light, but she didn't want to alert any neighbors or passing patrol cars.

She moved to the front window of the house and peeked out over the driveway. A police car drove to the front gates and stopped.

"Come up to the house. Come on." She taunted the police officer in a low voice. He was so far away that even if she yelled he still wouldn't be able to hear. She continued to stare at the officer as he aimlessly shone his flashlight to and fro. He didn't even move through the gates. A minute later, he was back in his vehicle and backing out of the entrance. She waited until the car was out of sight. If he bothered to come back at all tonight, it wouldn't be for another couple of hours. There was plenty of time.

Gretel wasn't worried. This was the routine patrol that Jack had mentioned. No wonder they needed her help if that was the best they could do.

She headed up the stairs taking them two at a time. Her heart pulsed hard with anticipation over what she'd discover in the safe. Visions of the Welch jewelry collection flashed before her. She loved the replica Egyptian jewelry crafted in the fifties by Serita, a major jewelry house. She was certain some of those pieces had made their way into Josephine's hands. Each piece was worth at least two hundred thousand.

As she pushed the study door open, it struck her that this robbery was too easy, too simple, and that was unnerving. Or maybe all residential robberies were this way.

The safe door was propped open. Convenient. She pulled down the blind, and then drew the curtain. Making her way back to the safe, she pulled out her flashlight, strapped it to her forehead and turned it on. The interior base was untouched, unopened. Without taking her eyes off the safe, she reached into her bag and pulled out the automatic screwdriver and proceeded to undo the screw in each corner. Then with the bent nail she'd brought with her, she pulled on the base and it came loose.

Second obstacle overcome.

After she lifted the base cover off, she couldn't believe what she saw illuminated by her flashlight.

It was empty.

Completely.

Nothing.

Lights outside distracted her. Immediately she flicked off her flashlight and ran to the window. Moving the blinds, she saw a car. It wasn't the patrol car. Then the front passenger door opened, and Gretel saw a woman. It had to be Mrs. Welch, home ahead of schedule. A man got out of the driver's door, his eyes scanning the house.

Gretel watched from the darkness above, sure Josephine and her companion wouldn't cross the crime scene tape. Then she heard the door open and muffled voices coming from downstairs. She was shocked.

Suddenly the house was lit inside and out like a football field at night.

There was no time to waste.

After she closed the heavy safe door, she spun the dial and realized she'd forgotten the four screws and the top plate that made the lid of the hidden section. Too late. She placed them between the wall and the safe. She sprinted halfway out the door, before she remembered she'd left her knapsack on the floor next to the safe. This wouldn't have happened if she'd taken precautions. Most times she had Kent as lookout, talking to her through an earpiece. She sprinted back to grab her stuff and heard voices. They were discussing that the security system was off and were concerned because they'd had it switched on remotely.

"Check the house." Gretel heard Mrs. Welch command. "Every inch of it."

"I'm on it. You wait right here," the man replied confidently, his voice raspy-sounding.

She took hold of her knapsack and ran to one of the bedrooms that lined the back of the house. She'd climb out the window and make her way down the sandstone blocks that made up the facade of the house.

When she got there, she found that it—and all the bedroom doors—was locked. That was something she hadn't planned for and there was no time to pick the locks. Someone was coming. Then she remembered from when she had visited there as a child, they had played on a servants' stairway that led to the kitchen. She raced to the corner and ran down the narrow stairs.

Arriving in the kitchen, she heard footsteps. She froze. Would she make it to the back door without being seen? She decided no, she wouldn't make it, and slipped into the butler's pantry and closed the door behind her.

When she heard closer footsteps on the kitchen floor, she knew it was the end. Would she be killed just like Mr. Welch? She backed further into the corner, but there was no place to hide. Feeling her heartbeats throbbing in her head, she picked up a knife ready to defend herself.

Then she placed it back, remembering her phone.

She'd been careless this time and over confident. She reached into the side pocket of her knapsack and pulled out her cell. Kent answered on the first ring. "I'm here and hiding in the Welch house. The owner's come home early, and I need them out now. Hurry. I'm hiding and they'll find me any minute."

"I'm on it."

She ended the call and shoved the phone into the pocket of her pants ready to run. Once more she picked up the knife and clutched the handle tightly. Moving to the door of the pantry, she heard the home phone. It was too close for comfort. The sounds rang out from the kitchen.

"Hello?" she heard. *A female voice, must be Mrs. Welch.* "Who is this? Is this a joke?" The receiver slammed down, and Mrs. Welch yelled out. "There's a bomb! We need to get out!"

Gretel heaved a sigh of relief as she listened to the scurrying footsteps, the slammed front door, and then the car driving away.

Get out of here fast!

She flung open the pantry door and ran to the back of the house.

"Stop!" someone called out.

Gretel froze with her hand on the door that led to the conservatory. Was it the police? She turned around and saw a dark figure with his hands by his sides. He appeared to have no weapon. Was it another thief with the same idea as she had? She wasn't going to wait around to find out. She ran through the doorway and sprinted across the backyard with the man now hot on her heels.

"Stop! I just want to talk."

She grabbed hold of the main hedge branch and from there started climbing using the metal fasteners as footholds. He was only inches from her when he started climbing too. He made a lunge and grabbed her leg. She kicked her leg trying to free herself from his grasp.

No!

She couldn't be caught.

Not like this.

CHAPTER 7

HANGING on to the fence for dear life, with an unknown man in black hanging on to her foot, she pulled her other leg up as high as she could and thrust it down at the man. It connected. She heard a yell as he fell back. Without looking down, she kept going, reaching up for the next handhold and the one above that.

Once she was on the top, she scrambled across, lowered herself and then let go and tumbled onto the ground to break her fall. From the backyard of the neighbor's property, she sprinted through to the street beyond. In case she was seen, she steadied her pace to a comfortable jog. She was dressed as though she was out for an evening jog, but for the knapsack on her back. Two streets away she came to her rental car and with no sign of the man in black, she knew she was safe.

She sat in the rental car breathing hard. There'd been not one close call, but two. After she called Kent and told him she was safe, she peeled off her pullover and then reality hit her again about how stupid she had been to be drawn in by temptation. When all was said and done, she'd just risked her freedom for an empty safe.

Gretel blew out a long deep breath. She hadn't made a contingency plan for Josephine returning and she certainly hadn't made one for coming face to face with another thief.

It hit her what would've happened if she'd gotten caught. It was stupid to take such a risk. But she hadn't gotten caught, and adrenaline pumped through every inch of her being. It was only in times like these that she felt truly alive.

It was then that she remembered the safe had been open when she got to it and she'd closed it. Hopefully, that would be a detail no one would notice.

She started the engine and then froze as she heard police sirens. After a minute, they stopped. Sounded like they'd just arrived at the Welches' house to investigate the bomb scare. Gretel smiled as she disengaged the handbrake and then she laughed out loud as she drove onward.

When Gretel was safely back in her apartment, the first thing she did was check her phone. Relief washed over her when she saw that there was no missed call from Jack asking where she was. *Phew!*

Still feeling pumped, she sank into the couch and her mind went over what had happened. Who was the man who'd been at the house with Josephine? If only she'd gotten a better look at him ... but she wouldn't forget his raspy voice.

What really bugged her now was the other man who'd appeared in the house after Josephine and her friend drove away. In her worst nightmares he'd be an investigator, or another thief come to find leftovers. Had he too suspected that the real jewelry hadn't been stolen and was still there?

Hours later, she woke up. She'd dozed off. She was still on the couch and in the same clothing. Now she was cold. A quick glance at her cell phone told her it was just after midnight. If Jack came uninvited into her apartment like he had the previous morning it wouldn't be good. She had to unpack her bag and get out of those clothes

After stripping off, she stepped into the shower. The hot water pummeled against her back, and her thoughts moved to her ex-boyfriend Ryan and where he was right now. It was a horrible feeling that he'd gotten the better of her. How could she have ever loved him? Why was her filter way off when it came to men? She was normally a good judge of character—had to be one in her line of work. He'd done a real number on her.

She turned off the water and reached for a towel. As she dried herself she had a dreadful thought. What if that man from the house knew who she was? The scene ran through her mind. She was pretty certain she'd be able to recognize him again if she heard his voice.

Once Gretel was in her usual nightly attire of a very unglamorous, over-sized t-shirt, she set about unpacking her burglar bag and hiding each item in its own spot. After that was done she felt better. Only thing was, now she was starving. Food would have to wait. She needed to talk to Kent about the man she'd just seen.

By the way he answered the phone she knew she'd woken him.

"What's up?"

She filled him in on the events of the previous evening, of how Josephine came to the house with a man, and then about the other man. "He had an athletic build, a little taller than me. He was somewhere in his forties, broad chiseled face, spoke in an educated and distinctly deep voice. I know what you're going to ask. Would I know him if I saw him again?"

"Would he know *you* if he saw *you* again?"

"I hope not. The house was dark, I was in black and I didn't speak. He tried to grab me. Well, he did grab me as I was climbing over the fence. It was a close call. Who do you think he was?"

"I don't know. I've got nothing to go on. I should've driven you, Gretel. You can't take a risk like that again no matter how easy you think it'll be."

"I can't think about that right now. That's in the past." She was already upset with herself for thinking it was going to be simple. Normally she was over-prepared. "What was he doing there? He was in the house while Josephine's friend was searching the place. He was hiding like I was. I never saw him when I was working on the safe, though."

"Was he going to jump you after you opened the safe for him?"

"No. It wasn't locked. The safe was unlocked but I had to unscrew the bottom plate to open the hidden compartment." She thought again of how she'd left the safe with that section uncovered and the loose bits between the safe and the wall. As soon as Josephine opened the safe she would see someone had been there.

"Do you think you were followed? Has Fletcher got a tail on you?"

"No. It's not possible. I made sure I wasn't followed to the car rental company and back home again. And I left my personal cell phone here in case he's tracking it."

"Maybe it's a waiting game. You might find out when you learn more about the Welch murder."

Gretel yawned. "I hope so. It's bugging me. Sorry for waking you up."

"That's okay. Night, Gretel."

"'Night?' Oh, it is still night. Goodnight, Kent."

After she ended the call, she opened the fridge and was faced with nothing but a chocolate bar and out of date orange juice. She'd had no time to shop.

The only thing in the cupboard, among the pasta and rice and other things that needed cooking, was a solitary can of vegetable soup. The funny thing was, she had no idea when she'd bought it or why. That wasn't unusual. She rarely ate at home and quite often had no idea what was lurking in her cupboard. Hunger forced her to open the can, dump the soup into a glass dish, and pop it into the microwave. While she waited for it to heat, she opted to toast some bread she found in the freezer.

It wasn't the best meal she'd ever had, but it beat prison food by a country mile.

GRETEL WAS DRAGGED from deep sleep by a loud knock on her door. From the apartment being flooded with light, she surmised it was morning. It had to be Jack Fletcher. Somehow, he'd managed to get past the doorman. Again. This was the third doorman they'd had in as many months and this one didn't seem to be any better than the others. Jack had probably flashed his badge, or flashed his smile. Either would work. Handsome people had such an advantage over others.

"Coming." She sat up and reached for her white

fluffy bathrobe that was on the other side of the bed. After she pulled it on, she stood up and hurried to the door finger-combing her hair into place. Once she confirmed from the security monitor it was Jack, she unlocked the door and opened it.

He walked past her with barely a look. "Last night there was an intruder in the Welch house."

Gretel closed the door behind him. There was no apology for waking her, no asking how she was, and no hello. All she could do was pretend concern over what he said. "That's dreadful. What happened?"

He turned around and looked her up and down.

"It's ten in the morning. Were you asleep?"

"Late night. Watching too much TV. Wait, wasn't there crime scene tape around the house?"

"Yes. They ignored that. It was a friend of Mr. and Mrs. Welch looking for Mrs Welch. Apparently, he was drunk and upset about what had happened to Mr. Welch. Fortunately we had the house on regular patrol by the local police. One of the patrol cars saw the lights in the house on, and called it in. They found his friend at the bottom of the driveway."

That must've been the intruder she'd seen. Maybe. "That was lucky. Did they get his name?"

"Yes."

"Test him for drunkenness?"

"He confessed he was drunk. There was no need."

"And, Josephine said she knew him?"

"Correct."

"What's his name?"

"I've got it written down somewhere."

The guy who grabbed her foot in the Welch garden had not been drunk at all. If Josephine knew him, maybe he was working for her. Perhaps an investigator like she had first thought. Or this was a different man altogether?

"We've got Mrs. Welch coming in today."

"So soon after her husband's been killed?"

"In a murder case time is of the essence. It mightn't be the best timing for the family but it's our best chance of finding the killer. Then the family can have closure."

"Closure is good." She nodded, and then looked down at herself. "I guess I should get changed."

"Yes, and hurry."

"While I'm doing that do you want to make yourself some coffee?"

"Sure. You want one?"

"Yes, please," she called over her shoulder as she headed to her room. Intending to put a proper effort into helping Jack with his case, she decided on her most conservative outfit. A pencil-thin cream skirt with a black blouse, and black pumps. No jewelry.

She pulled a brush through her hair and did her makeup as fast as she could. It didn't seem like Jack was a patient man and she didn't want to keep him waiting.

When she walked out, he saw her and raised his eyebrows.

His face said, 'Wow,' even though he didn't utter a word. Then he looked down at something in his hand.

"What have you got there?" she asked.

He passed her a coffee and then opened his other hand to reveal a wrapped candy, a promotional give-away item from the rental car company.

Her heart nearly stopped. Why had she taken it? And how stupid to leave it lying about like that?

She thought fast. Fixing a smile on her face, she snatched it from him and then threw it in the kitchen waste bin. "I'm trying to stay off sugar. It's a hard habit to break." She giggled. "Someone was giving those away in the street yesterday. Not sure why I took one."

He took a sip of coffee while staring at her. "Yes, sugar's a hard habit to break."

"Tell me about it." She hoped he believed her and wouldn't remember which rental car company it was from. *Good luck with that,* she told herself. *It's likely seared into his memory.*

LATER THAT MORNING at the FBI interview area, Mrs. Welch walked in with a man she introduced as her brother-in-law, Reginald Welch, who was also a lawyer. When Gretel heard his raspy-toned voice, she knew without a doubt he was the man who'd accompanied

Josephine to her house last night. Being a lawyer, he'd positively know better than to cross crime scene tape. That told her he wasn't the most upstanding lawyer in town.

While Jack interviewed Josephine, Gretel listened from the other room. It was then Gretel realized Josephine had lived most of her life surrounded by lawyers, with both her first and second husbands being lawyers. And now her brother-in-law.

After a half-hour-long interview, with Reginald stopping his sister-in-law from answering practically every other question, Jack excused himself and walked into the adjoining room where Gretel had been listening.

He leaned against the door and locked eyes with her. Slowly he walked forward and sat on a desk close to her. "What do you think?"

"She's guilty. She killed him, took the jewels, and aims to pocket the insurance money too."

His lips twisted into a smirk. "What makes you say that?"

"Just a feeling."

"I tend to agree with you, but we'll need evidence."

"Why does she need a lawyer? I mean, isn't she trying to help you?"

"She's just being cautious. Her lawyer knows we look at the family first when there's a murder."

Gretel nodded. "They must know you doubt the whole story about the intruders killing Glen Welch."

"Maybe they do." He looked down at his shoes and then looked back at her. "If she's guilty, that means there was no robbery. Where would she have hidden the jewels?"

"Could be anywhere. She had someone else do the job – the pretend robbery and the killing. The jewelry could be anywhere. Maybe even still in the house somewhere." Her mind was drawn back to the other man, the one hiding in the house.

"I'll get a warrant and have the house searched from top to bottom."

"I know you're good at your job and everything, but I don't think you'll ever find who killed him. The person who did the actual killing."

"Why?"

She shrugged her shoulders. "Could be anyone, and by now they could be anywhere. Bermuda, Honduras, Dubai, Paris."

"We will get them. We'll see what the forensics have to say. Be more positive, Gretel. We usually get our man."

Gretel wished she could say the same. The only man she'd gotten was a useless, lying, double-crossing rat. Looking back through the glass at Josephine, her gaze drifted to Reginald, the brother-in-law lawyer. Why had he been with Josephine at the house? "Okay, sure. I'll try to be more positive, Jack."

"That's the way." He took one of the three bottles of water on the table and passed her one. When she shook her head, he unscrewed the cap and took a mouthful. "Time to go back in and ask some more questions."

"Good luck."

CHAPTER 8

LATER IN THE DAY, Jack and Gretel sat down in Jack's sparsely furnished office. As she waited for him to check his emails, she noticed how neatly the files on his long desk were arranged into two groups. Two filing cabinets stood by the narrow window while the only thing adorning the gray walls was a large corkboard with notes pinned to it. The lack of personal mementos and family photographs reinforced her opinion of him being all work and no play.

Then he said, "Done," and looked at her. "We're going to have to check in with all the local fences."

It surprised her that they'd have to do the groundwork like that. He was a *special* agent after all. "Wouldn't the underdog cops do that stuff?"

His head tilted to one side as he clasped his hands together and rested them on his desk. "What do you mean by 'underdog cops?'"

"Well, you're a 'special agent.' So don't you have other people, 'not-so-special agents,' to do things like that? Or just send out a memo?"

"I'm not talking about going to see any leads that *I* know. I'm talking about the fences that *you* might know."

The words were delivered like a knife to the heart. Immediately Gretel was sick to the stomach. Did he think she was going to be an informant? She would never reveal the people she'd worked with. "Look, that was never the deal. It's not something I can do."

"You help me, and I help you. One hand washes the other—"

She interrupted quickly, knowing his next words would be that he could always send her back to the prison she'd escaped from. "Yes, but I'm not helping you so much that I'll get myself killed."

"Just as well I have someone who's called in. He's given us information before. Not me personally but people I work with. You might know him. Herman Smythe."

She was relieved. He'd been seeing how far he could push her. "I've never heard of him," she lied. Herman Smythe was a low-level fence. She knew of him, but she'd never worked with him. He'd never be able to move the kind of goods that she dealt in.

"Well, we're on the way to see him." He bounded to his feet.

Looking up at him, she asked. "Right now? Aren't you going to finish talking to Mrs.—"

Jack's eyes bore into hers. "It's under control. Unless you have something better to do?"

She looked at her nails. "I need time off to attend to a few personal things. I have to get my nails done." More important than needing her nails done or visiting the hairdresser was finding her rotten ex-boyfriend. Where was she going to find time for that? Even though she had Kent on the job, it annoyed her that she couldn't do anything to help. Jack was taking up all her time.

He didn't look pleased with her. "There'll be plenty of time for your nails once we have Welch's killer behind bars."

Out of frustration she bit the inside of her mouth.

"Once we locate your boyfriend and the diamonds you say he has, and then find out who killed Glen Welch and stole the jewelry, you can have all the pedicures you want. But right now we've got things to do."

She smiled at him not knowing the difference between a manicure and a pedicure. "I won't argue with that. I could use a pedicure, too."

He narrowed his eyes, and then he looked over at the door.

Gretel turned around to see him looking at a very attractive woman who was smirking at him. Straight blonde hair stopped bluntly at her shoulders and she wore a figure-hugging skirt with matching jacket. Her blouse was undone way too far.

"Just stopped by to see if you wanted help on the Welch case."

"No, it's under control, thanks."

She folded her arms and walked further into his office, looking at Gretel. "Who do we have here?"

Gretel stood up and reached out her hand. "Gretel Koch."

"Gretel's working with us. Gretel, meet Monica."

"Hello, Monica," Gretel said, letting her arm drop down by her side when the woman ignored it. She'd only glanced at her before her gaze swept back to Jack.

"I heard about her coming here and I thought it was a joke."

"It's not a joke, Monica," Jack said.

Monica shook her head, still staring at Jack. "I've just wrapped up my case, so if you need help, you better be quick."

"I'll keep that in mind."

She smiled at him and then shot a frosty look at Gretel before she walked out the door.

"Wow." Gretel couldn't believe how rude the woman had been. "Who was that?"

"Monica Blaze, one of the agents. I'm sorry about that. She is a good agent believe it or not. Let's go."

They walked out of his office to the elevator. The last office on the left side of the corridor was Monica's, Gretel noticed. She'd have to keep an eye on that one.

HALF AN HOUR LATER, Gretel Koch and Jack Fletcher walked into Herman Smythe's pawnshop. There was only one man behind the counter, a bald-headed guy with well-muscled, hairy arms and wearing an assortment of gold bracelets and heavy gold neck chains. The diamonds in the square ring on his pinkie sparkled. He was the typical man you'd need working in a pawn shop to deal with the many disgruntled customers coming in to collect their goods past the due date. "Is Herman Smythe in?"

"Who wants to know?"

"Jack Fletcher. I called this morning, he's expecting us."

"He didn't mention it, but that doesn't mean nuthin'." He looked from Jack to Gretel and back to Jack. He picked up a phone's receiver and pressed a button and said a few words to Herman, while Gretel had a casual look around observing the security. When he ended the call, he looked up. "Come this way."

They followed him through to the back. "Second door on the left."

Jack knocked. "Jack Fletcher and associate here."

"Come in."

They walked into his room. A small skinny man sat behind a large desk with various instruments and weighing scales strewn over it. "Nice to meet you." He leaned across the desk offering his hand. Jack shook it and then Gretel offered her hand and he shook it looking into her eyes. "Have a seat."

Once they were seated, Jack said, "Thank you for seeing us."

"How can I help you?" Before Jack could answer he looked at Gretel and pointed at her. "I know you."

"Oh." Gretel didn't know what to say. She'd never met him, only heard about him.

"You're Gretel Koch."

"Yes, she is," Jack answered, "and she's helping us with a few things. You told one of my associates you had information about the recent robbery at the Welch home. I'm guessing you heard Glen Welch was murdered and his home robbed?"

Gretel was grateful Jack had steered the attention away from her.

Smythe licked his lips and leaned back in his chair. "Yes. I heard. None of their jewelry has come here. I'd know if it had. We got an email alert yesterday listing the stolen items."

"So, what do you know?"

Then he moved closer to them. So close that Gretel could smell the alcohol on him. "There was a similar robbery months back. The man wasn't killed, but it sounds like it might've been the same crew."

"How was it similar?" Gretel doubted what he said. He was clearly not one to be trusted.

"He was left for dead on the floor in front of his safe. They took everything."

Jack pulled a notepad and pen from his inner jacket pocket and then clicked on the end of his pen as he flipped the notepad open. "Name? I'll look it up on the system."

"There won't be anything to look up about it."

Jack paused to stare at him. "Why do you say that?"

"He never reported it to the cops. The goods weren't come by the right way if you know what I mean. And you didn't hear that from me."

Gretel sensed Jack was getting frustrated. "How long ago did this happen?"

"Few weeks."

Jack frowned. "How badly was he hurt?"

"He was pretty badly banged up."

"Name?" Jack repeated. "He could know something that would help. Even if it's something small."

"I'll tell you." He picked up his phone and scrolled through it. "Ramsey Goldbloom. I can give you a phone number, but on the way out, you'll have to ask Pete for his address." He picked up his phone's receiver, pressed a number, and then asked Pete to have Goldbloom's address ready. He replaced the receiver and looked over at them. "That's all I can help you with. If I hear of anything else, I'll let you know."

That was his polite way of asking them to leave.

After they collected the address from Pete, they headed out of the shop.

"That was awful. He recognized me. I wasn't happy about that."

"You might have to get used to that. You caused quite a sensation."

"Something best avoided. That's always been my policy. Lay low, keep out of the spotlight. Thanks to you arresting me that's all gone by the wayside."

"I just need to make a few calls." He nodded to a café. "Order me a coffee and something to eat and I'll be over in a minute." He passed her a fifty. "Get yourself something too, of course."

"Is this breakfast?"

"I haven't eaten today if that's what you mean."

She smiled at him and then headed to the café. Hanging out with Jack was far better than being in jail, and it also kept her mind off Ryan who was probably long gone by now. Although, it wasn't exactly helping to keep her on the straight and narrow.

She made a food and drink order and then sat at a table and waited for him.

Sitting by the window and looking out, she watched him pace up and down talking on the phone. He certainly was handsome. Was he married? He didn't wear a ring, but some men didn't. As she'd observed that morning, there were no signs of a wife in his office. Nothing would ever happen between them. Not when he saw her as a criminal. Still, she could dream.

He ended his call and walked into the café. When he'd sat down across from her, he said, "I found out he came in there with a concussion, and he had some pretty serious cuts and abrasions."

"Excuse me? Who are we talking about?"

He frowned at her. "Ramsey Goldbloom."

"Ah. You confused me when you said, 'came in there.' Did you mean he went to a hospital?"

"Yes. I'm sorry, Gretel. I tend to think people know what's going on in my head. We were just talking about him. Anyway, he'd been knocked out cold. Nothing was reported to the police. He told the hospital he'd fallen down some stairs and his head hit the banister on the way down."

"Ah, good work getting the info from the hospital."

He gave half a smile. The waitress brought their coffees over and said their food wouldn't be long.

"What are we eating?" he asked Gretel.

"Toasted sandwiches. I hope that's all right. I didn't know what to get you." She pushed the change over to him.

He took it, shoving it all in a pocket. "Thanks. Sandwiches are fine. Anything's fine. I'm not a fussy eater."

"I'm guessing we're heading to see Ramsey Goldbloom after this?"

"Ah, you remembered his name. I was getting worried about you for a moment."

"I do have a good memory for names."

"We're meeting him in an hour. He thinks we want to talk to him about his hospital visit. He owns a car wash not far from here."

The first thing that sparked in her mind when she heard the words 'car wash' was money laundering.

CHAPTER 9

GRETEL AND JACK sat opposite Ramsey Goldbloom in his office. He had to be in his early thirties, Gretel surmised. She'd expected to see someone older. His dark eyes were hiding something, she was sure of it. He ran a hand through his thick woolly hair.

Jack came right to the point and told Goldbloom he'd heard about the robbery and didn't believe the story Ramsey had given the hospital.

A pained expression glazed over Goldbloom's face as his lips pulled to one side. "I didn't report it because, to start with, they weren't my goods. I was holding on to 'em for a friend."

"Always a friend," Jack said matter-of-factly.

"It's true. A friend asked me to hold a bag for him for a couple weeks. I didn't ask questions and I didn't even know what was in there, know what I mean?" Ramsey shrugged his shoulders, crumpling his cheap

65

navy suit. "When I told him what had happened, he said they must've followed him and then he told me what was in the bag. He admitted it was jewelry and it was hot."

Gretel stared at the man. Did he really expect them to believe he never once looked in the bag?

"Who's your friend?" Jack asked.

"I can't tell you that."

Jack leaned forward showing his patience was wearing thin. "Who did your friend think was after him?"

"A group of people who steal from people who've stolen. They must've been, since he said that, know what I mean?"

"And the name of your friend?" Jack asked once more.

He shook his head. "I'm sorry I can't say. I've already told you more than I wanted to."

"Did he say anything else?" Gretel asked.

"Only that he called them 'The Shadows.' That's all he said."

Jack gazed at him in a most patient manner and she could tell that was his way of making the man nervous. Finally, he asked, "Are you telling us stories?"

"Nah, it's all true." He shifted in his seat. "That's exactly what he said."

"He must've been upset about the ... The Shadows taking his stuff," Gretel said, half glancing at Jack, who wasn't looking too happy. It sounded to her like this guy had been watching too many movies.

"He hasn't talked to me since. I was pretty banged up. That helped him not be too mad at me I'd reckon."

"Is this Shadows gang well known among your … associates?"

"All I did was help him as a one-off thing. I don't know any criminals. Know what I mean? I run a legit car wash business as you can see."

Gretel was surer than ever the car wash was a money-laundering operation. She'd noticed they had a sign up that they only took cash. That was unusual to say the least. "Who did your friend think was behind The Shadows?"

"He said it was run by the big guys. He said something like, they let the little guys steal and they step in and take it from 'em, know what I mean?"

Gretel decided to count how many times he said *know what I mean*. She was sorry she hadn't started counting from the beginning.

"What did these men look like?" Jack asked.

"Dunno. They wore black ski masks. They were big, tall." He made Hulk-like motions with his arms to show they were muscular.

"Did any of them have an accent?" Jack asked.

"No. They spoke like regular folk. Mean, regular folk."

Gretel thought back to the man she'd seen in the Welches' house. He'd been alone, though. Then there were the two men searching Ryan's hotel room while she was hiding in the closet moments before Jack had arrested her after her prison escape. Were those men The Shadows? She assumed there had been two of them because she only heard two voices. One of them called the other, 'Monzo.' "Did you hear any names mentioned?" Gretel asked him.

Goldbloom looked at her. "Huh?"

"Did one of them call the other a certain name? Frank, John, Dave?"

He shook his head. "Nah. I'd like to help ya more, but that's all I got." He opened his drawer and pulled out a couple of vouchers. "Here. Get ya cars washed on me. One each."

"Thank you." Gretel leaned forward and took hers.

Jack shook his head and held up his hand.

Gretel reached for Jack's voucher. "I'll take his."

Jack put his hand over hers, and then plucked the vouchers away. "We can't take anything, Gretel." He pushed the vouchers back across the desk. "I'm sorry."

"No worries. It wasn't a bribe. Got nothin' to bribe ya over."

"I know, but all the same. Thank you for the offer."

On the way out of the building, Jack explained, "We can't take anything that could be seen as a bribe."

"It was just a car wash."

"It doesn't matter. We can't be seen to take anything or be given anything."

She nodded. "Noted. I do like free things, though.

Something for nothing. I mean, who doesn't, know what I mean?"

He stared at her and then shook his head. "Don't."

Gretel laughed.

As they continued to his car, he said, "Can't you afford to get your car washed, Gretel? I thought the interior design business was doing well."

"It was, but I've since retired so …" According to the IRS she had an interior design business. That's how she got her money. She didn't know the FBI could look into her tax records. They might have subpoenaed them. "I don't like to pass up something for free." She gave him a bright smile so he wouldn't see she was disturbed by him knowing her fake personal details.

Once they were in the car, he looked at his phone. "There's not much to do until I get the forensic reports."

"How long will that take?"

"Some will take weeks, others might be back as soon as tomorrow. This afternoon will be taken up with interviewing family members." Then he smiled at her. "That manicure might have to wait."

"I'm fine with that. I'm anxious to hear what they have to say. I wonder if you'll crack someone by your rocking interviewing technique and they'll confess."

His lips curved upward slightly. "It has happened before. Today we've got the brother, the stepdaughter, and Greeves, the business partner. Tomorrow it's the two full-time staff, the regular cleaners, and the company that maintains the gardens."

"Can't wait."

GRETEL SAT in the room adjoining the interview room, the same place she'd sat for the last two days. Jack was no closer to finding out who killed Glen Welch. For Gretel, it was all a big waste of time and Ryan Castle had a huge head start.

Jack finished his last interview for the day and walked into the room with her. "I just got a message that Glen Welch's body has been released to the family. How would you like to go somewhere with me?"

Her heart raced. Was he asking her on a date? The expression on his handsome face gave nothing away. He'd done nothing to show her he was interested in her as a woman. "Go where?" she managed to say, doing her absolute best to hide the freak-out that was going on in her head.

"Dust off your black dress, we're going to a funeral."

"A funeral?" That was disappointing. Who was she kidding? He was too straight to be interested in a woman like her. A woman with a sordid and criminal past.

"Yes, a funeral."

Funeral? That was so far from the date for which she was hoping. "When will it be?"

"Sometime within the next week I'd say."

It meant being out in public and possibly photographed. "I can't go. My parents are sure to be there. My sister is a good friend of Gizelle's and my parents are probably still friends with Josephine. Maybe not friends, but associates—someone my parents took money from for their church."

"I think it's time you made amends with your parents."

Gretel drew in a quick breath at the thought. "You know nothing about them." What she really meant was that he didn't know how horrible they were. Sure, everyone thought her parents were the perfect Christian couple with the perfect family, but they weren't. They were mean and cruel. They'd never treated her with love or shown her any understanding. All they did was judge her.

"They might know something useful about this case."

NO! she screamed in her head. "No. They wouldn't. They only know how to take money from people. You should see how much they rake in when they go on their tours." They took money for their ministry and paid themselves a hefty wage. It wasn't right, and they called *her* a criminal.

"I'm sure it all goes where it's supposed to, or they wouldn't have lasted this long. Why not make a move to bridge the gap?"

"I might." Yes, she *might* go to the house on Sunday

when they were sure to be in church. Her sister, Hazel, would be there and she'd find out if her folks were planning to go to Mr. Welch's funeral. "I'll see what I can do."

"Good girl."

Good girl? Who did he think he was talking to? A trained pet? Maybe she was merely a project to him.

CHAPTER 10

GRETEL'S FAMILY'S first church service of the day started at ten, so that was when Gretel arrived at her old family home on Sunday. She was pleased that Hazel answered the door since she hadn't told her she'd be coming.

"You're home," Gretel said when Hazel answered the door.

"Yes. What are you doing here?" She grabbed Gretel and hugged her. "I'm so pleased you're out and out for good."

"Me too. Thanks again for your help."

"Of course. I'm glad it all worked out. So, what are you doing here?" she asked again. "You haven't been here for years."

"I could ask you the same thing. I thought you'd be out with your boyfriend on a nice day like this. What's his name again?"

"Jason. We broke up. I told you that when I visited you in prison."

Gretel put her hand to her head. She did recall her sister telling her that. "Ah, sorry; I forgot. I had a few things on my mind back then."

"I was just about to put a face mask on. Want to join me?"

"Sure." They headed to the bathroom where Hazel had a gooey green lotion ready. Gretel picked up the brush and mixed it around. "And this is?"

"A mixture of green tea, vitamin C, Aloe Vera, and a few other things. I made it myself."

"Hmm. Interesting." She leaned down and sniffed it. "Smells okay."

"You'll need to take off your makeup." She handed Gretel a facial wipe.

As she cleaned her face, Hazel applied the green goo to her own face.

"You heard about what happened to Glen Welch?" Gretel asked.

"Yes. It's so awful."

"I know. The FBI has me helping them with it. Don't tell anyone."

"Oh, that's exciting. I won't tell anyone. You live such an exciting life and you're so lucky they're keeping you out of prison. Do they know who did it yet?"

"Not yet." She couldn't wait any longer. "Are Mom and Dad going to Welch's funeral?"

"They can't. They're leaving tomorrow for a ministry cruise."

That was the best news she'd had for a while. It was a weight off her shoulders. "Ministry Cruise? That's a new one."

Hazel kept applying 'green goo' to her face. "It's a new thing they've started. People will go along to enjoy the cruise and take part in daily worship sessions where they can grow closer to God."

"How nice for them."

Hazel giggled. "Don't be sarcastic."

"I'm not."

Hazel handed her the green, goo-filled brush. "Here you go. Don't go close to your eyes 'cuz it'll tighten a lot."

Standing next to her sister, Gretel brushed the concoction over her face.

"How does it feel?"

Gretel puffed out her cheeks. "It's tightening already."

"Yes, it's good. Now we have to lie on the floor with our feet elevated."

Hazel raced out of the room and Gretel followed reminded of all the fun they had when they were younger. They lay down on the living room floor with their feet on the couch.

"Just don't get any goo on the rug or Mom will kill us."

"No she won't because she won't know I've been here. She might kill you."

"You should wait for them to get home. They haven't seen you in ages."

"Don't tell them I was here. I'll be long gone by the time they come home. They could've come to see me in jail, but they didn't bother."

"They were shocked, that's why. They thought you were a decorator. Choosing lamps for people and that kind of thing."

Gretel tried to smile at their stupidity, but the mask was too tight and hurt her face.

Hazel continued, "I couldn't believe it when you told me about the FBI. It's a dream come true and shows you that prayers work."

"Prayers? I didn't think you believed in all that."

"Well, even you'd have to believe it was a miracle. Everyone prayed. They still pray for you. You would've been convicted for sure if you'd had a trial."

"We'll never know." Gretel preferred not to think about it. "It's in the past." She could not entertain the ludicrous thought that it was prayer that got her out of prison. It was her own ingenuity, with a dash of help from several people, and a good dollop of luck.

"I'm not out of trouble just yet. Not completely. I still don't have any real assurances that I won't be deported to some foreign country to stand trial. Bolivia, France, England, Russia."

"No, I don't think Russia has an extradition treaty with us."

"Probably not, but I don't feel safe either way, not really."

"I'm sure you're out of danger."

"For now, hopefully," Gretel murmured to herself. "I hope it stays that way."

"Why wouldn't it? Wait a minute, why are you here?"

"Because I knew our lovely parents would be at work – or should I say church? – scamming people for donations, and I wanted to see you."

"That's not what they do, Gretel. They're doing the Lord's work. They are genuine you know."

"Genuinely stupid if they expect people to believe all that. I needed to find out if Mom and Dad planned to go to Mr. Welch's funeral. And I found out."

"They'll be gone for three weeks on the cruise."

"Good. Excellent." Gretel patted her cheeks. "How long do we leave this on?"

"A little while longer if you want your pores cleaned out."

"I do. They've been through a lot."

"Tell me about your detective friend," asked Hazel.

"No, and he's not a detective, he's a special agent. Also, he's not a friend. You can trust friends and I don't trust him."

Hazel giggled. "Tell me about him anyway."

"There's nothing to tell. He offered me a lifeline and

I took it. End of story." Gretel didn't want to waste time talking about herself. What she needed was information. Since Gizelle was a good friend of Hazel's it was a perfect chance to get intel. "How's Gizelle holding up about her stepfather?"

"Is that why you're here, just to ask me about Gizelle?"

Now she felt bad. "I wanted to see you. I know you've probably been past my place to see me since I've been out, but I've not been home much."

"Mom told me to stay away from you, so I haven't stopped by to see you."

"Oh. Nice."

"Don't be mad at her, Gretel."

"She never did like me. I'm not mad. I'm over it." *Focus Gretel,* she told herself. It wasn't the time to think about her horrible childhood. "I was just asking about Gizelle because I was there when she was interviewed. Not there in the room, but listening in. Don't tell anyone that." Gretel knew she could trust her sister with secrets.

"I won't tell anyone. I haven't even seen Gizelle, but I did speak to her on the phone. She's dreadfully upset. What have you found out about Mr. Welch? I didn't like to ask her too much about what happened. I read in the papers he interrupted a robbery and that's how he was killed."

In an effort to garner more information, Gretel gave her sister some things to think about. "I'm sure he was murdered and it was made to look like a robbery. I don't believe there were intruders. That's what I think."

Hazel gasped. "Really? Who would've done that? Do you think Josephine killed him?"

Gretel was surprised by Hazel's response. She must know more about Josephine. Gizelle must've said something. "Why do you say Josephine?"

"No reason, really. I just thought that you thought that."

"I'm not sure. It could've been any number of people, but the first suspect has to be Mrs. Welch. She gets rid of her boring old husband, gets the insurance money from the jewelry, and gets to keep the jewelry too, if it wasn't really stolen."

"Back up a moment. Why would she want to get rid of her husband?"

"I don't know. He was probably annoying. She was probably sick of him after however many years of marriage. Wouldn't you hate the sight of someone after living with them for years?"

Hazel pouted. "Not if I was in love with him."

"Yeah well, love's not all it's cracked up to be. Love is only in fairy tales. It's not real."

"You never change, Gretel." Hazel giggled. "You don't believe in love or God. What do you believe in?"

"Myself."

Hazel giggled again.

Gretel sat up. "I have to get this thing off my face.

It's getting so tight it's giving me claustrophobia. Okay?"

They headed to the bathroom where they both washed their faces at the double basins.

"There, isn't that better?"

Gretel wiped her face dry with a towel and then stared into the mirror. "Yes. It does look refreshed." She couldn't see any difference. "I'm going to check out my old room while I'm here." She wandered into her old room expecting to see it the same, with all her things around. When she pushed the door open, she was shocked. It'd been turned into a guest bedroom with floral wallpaper and a green bedspread. Gone were her gymnastic trophies and her running medals, along with her collection of teddies that had sat atop a high shelf. The shelf wasn't even there anymore. What else would she expect from them? She lowered herself heavily on the bed and then Hazel walked in and saw her face.

"They've only done this recently. You never come here, so that's why they did this. Your things are still here. They didn't throw them out."

Gretel was even more disappointed in her parents. "I'm guessing all my things are in the garage stored in plastic crates."

"Probably."

"Your bedroom would be the same as it always was. You're the favorite."

"No I'm not. They don't even remember my name half the time."

Gretel smiled. "Still, you're more favorite than me."

"That's only because they know you hate them, and I never left home. Just the once but I was back before they could even think about redecorating."

Gretel bounded to her feet. Being there was bringing her down. "I should go."

Hazel grabbed her arm. "No stay."

"I can't. I've got so many things to do." She walked out to the living room and grabbed her bag and keys.

"Stay, Gretel," Hazel whined. "They won't be home for hours."

"I know, but I've got to catch up with things." She leaned forward and hugged Hazel. "I'll call you and we'll do lunch, okay?"

"I'd like that."

As soon as Gretel was back in her car, she called Kent. "Have you found out anything?"

"Marty still hasn't heard of anyone that meets Ryan's description looking for a new ID."

It was a long shot. IDs weren't that hard to come by.

Kent continued, "No one knows anything about The Shadow group, or gang. Sounds like a bunch of superheroes."

"I know. That's what I thought. I wonder if he's trying to throw us off the track. Thanks anyway. I guess it's a waiting game now. Waiting for Ryan to put a foot wrong."

"And he will. No one can hide forever. I've got all my checks in place. If he makes one move, I'll locate him."

"Thanks. Call me the moment he does." Gretel ended the call.

On her way home, she drove slowly past Ryan's apartment. She was tempted to go in to take a look around. Was he hiding the diamonds in plain sight like she continued to hide goods in her apartment?

She pressed her foot on the gas. It wasn't worth it. Someone was sure to see her, and the police would find out she'd been there. She didn't want to make another silly move that could come to nothing or get her in trouble.

It still ate away at her that someone she'd loved had wronged her. The worst thing was that he was gone, and she couldn't even yell at him or tell him how upset she was. He'd played her for a fool.

Weaving her car in and out of traffic, her mind drifted to the last time she'd seen Ryan. At that time she knew what he'd done. He was at the airport lying on the ground shot by airport security. She had to leave him there not knowing whether he was going to live or die. He'd said the diamonds were in a picture frame, but he lied. When she got to the place where he'd been staying, they weren't in the picture frame. Why was she shocked about him lying? That was all he seemed to do.

A car horn blasting at her when she cut across traffic brought her attention back to the present. To keep going and keep focused, she had to eliminate her obsession with being upset about Ryan. That wasn't going to be easy but she had to shelve those hurts and concentrate on getting those diamonds back. This was business and not personal.

CHAPTER 11

FOR GLEN WELCH'S FUNERAL, Gretel had gone shopping. She bought a blonde wig and, in case that wasn't enough to keep her identity masked, she bought a broad-brimmed hat. Black with a band of white trim —a perfect funeral hat.

Gretel hated funerals and avoided them whenever she could, but for some reason her new boss insisted she attend. She pulled her hair into the hairnet, and then pulled on the wig. It was realistic, she thought as she adjusted it in the mirror. No one would be able to tell it wasn't her natural hair unless they already knew her and had seen her own hair, which was sometimes black, red, or chestnut brown depending on her mood.

Thankfully, her parents weren't going to be at the funeral. That was one good thing about the day. Standing back from the mirror in the bathroom she studied herself. Then she slipped on her dark glasses.

She looked like she was about to attend a somber event, but she wasn't so sure the bright red lipstick was appropriate. *No, definitely not.* She opened the drawer and pulled out a moist towelette and wiped it off. Then she chose a light pink blush shade. Far more appropriate.

Her cell phone sounded.

She looked at the caller ID. It was Jack. "Yes, boss."

He hesitated. It was the first time she'd called him boss out loud. "I'm downstairs."

"I'm coming." She ended the call. Before she left, she stopped at the mirror in her changing room. The black dress clung to her figure and finished at the knee. It was conservative enough without being dowdy. Lastly, she grabbed a black coat and slung it over her arm.

When she got downstairs, she was looking for Jack's car and couldn't see it anywhere and then she saw someone waving at her—Jack, standing beside a black car.

She walked over and Jack opened her door with a long sideways look. "Not very funereally. A bombshell in black. I nearly didn't know it was you."

"Good, I think." She held her hat, and slid into the front seat, and he closed the door and walked around to get in the other side.

He moved the car into traffic.

"You think I'm a bombshell?" she asked grinning.

"I didn't say that, exactly."

"You did."

He smiled. "I didn't mean it." He was always in control—so in control of everything. "I see you brought a coat?" he asked.

"There's a cool change forecast."

"Wear it, please. That dress is far too figure hugging. I don't want us to get too much attention."

Neither did she want attention. In fact, she would rather stay at home, and she nearly told him so. "I can always wait in the car."

"You won't be any good to me in the car. I'll need you to keep your eyes and ears open. I'm sure the killer will be in the church somewhere. And, do you need to wear that hat? I can hardly see your face."

"That's the point of it, and see?" She moved her hat back slightly so he could see her blonde hair.

"That wasn't necessary, was it?"

"Was for me. At least my parents won't be there. That's a good thing."

"They didn't know him that well?"

"They knew him well enough to go, but they're off on one of their evangelistic missions around the country. No wait, it's a cruise this time."

"You don't look so sad that they can't be there."

"You know I'm not. There's no love lost between us."

"That's sad."

From his comment, she knew he must've been close to his family. "That's just the way things are. It doesn't bother me. They gave up on me a long time ago, so I eventually gave up on them."

"Well, you can hardly blame them. You weren't exactly a shining light for them. Someone they could boast about."

"Thanks very much."

He laughed. "It's true."

"They have plenty of other children to boast about. My older brother even went into the ministry."

"And you don't talk to him either, I'm guessing."

"Exactly. What are you doing about Ryan?"

"I told you. I've got people on it."

"Well, what are they doing exactly?" She didn't want to keep harping on it, but she needed to know.

"Trust me, it's under control. We're doing everything we can."

Gretel hated that she was thinking about Ryan all the time. "I hope you believe that I don't have those diamonds."

"I do, Gretel. And I'll help you clear your name."

She lifted the side of her hat to look at his handsome face and saw him smiling. "Good. Thank you." She couldn't help it when tingles traveled through her body.

Jack parked two blocks from the church. The crowd around the chapel was ridiculous. "This is all for Welch?" he asked as they both got out of the car.

"It looks that way." Gretel held onto her hat as a

cool breeze swept up. She was glad she'd brought the coat.

"I had no idea it was going to be this big."

"He was a wealthy man and knew a lot of people."

"I know, but still, I wasn't prepared."

"Now do you know why I wore this hat?"

He frowned at her. "Not really."

"Anonymity."

He tilted his head to the side. "You'll attract more attention with the size of it."

"I don't think so." She nodded her head at a group of ladies outside the church with hats just as big.

He looked over at them. "Maybe you're right. You'll fit right in."

As they got closer, she spotted a familiar figure. It was her main fence, Jackson Forsitto. He owned a prestige jewelry store in the heart of the city. Because he had so many contacts, he was able to move things other people couldn't. He'd connected her with people overseas and he was a vital part of her operation. She immediately looked away from him. They couldn't acknowledge each other.

"Is he someone you know?" Jack asked, having noticed her gaze pause at Forsitto.

She shook her head, concerned that her eyes had lingered on him for too long. "No. I mean, I see people in the society pages that I recognize. But I don't know any of these people personally."

"That's right. Your job wouldn't allow you to mix well with those kinds of people."

"That's right." She deliberately calmed her breathing, hoping she'd diverted his attention from Forsitto.

"Tell me again, what is it you do for your day job?"

"I'm an interior designer." She was, according to her financials in case she was ever audited.

"That's right. You file tax returns."

"Of course I do. Everybody is required to do that."

"You must have a good accountant."

"He is a good one." To avoid causing her accountant grief, she added, "I give him the figures of what I've made, and my outgoings and he does the rest."

"Fair enough. Don't worry I'm not going after your accountant." He looked around. "I think every lawyer in town is here. We should go in."

As they walked through the front doors of the memorial chapel, she said, "Can we sit in the back?"

"I usually do." They slid into the back pew and moved halfway along. "This way I'll get to keep an eye on everyone."

"That was my reasoning." Gretel took a moment to look around the church. "It's so pretty isn't it?"

"It is nice. Is this the first time you've been here?"

"As far as I can remember." She looked around at the pale blue walls and white archways.

Then Gretel noticed Glen Welch's business partner, Doug Greeves was sitting to the left of Gizelle and her mother in the front row. Sitting at Josephine's right was her brother-in-law, Reginald.

Josephine took out a tissue and dabbed at her eyes.

Jack whispered to Gretel, "I don't like funerals."

"Me either." She wanted to suggest they leave, but she knew he wouldn't. While she sat, she wondered about the victim's money. He was wealthy before he married Josephine and she was wealthy too, so added together they were able to splurge on jewelry. Why had his firm suddenly taken a downward turn?

When she saw Jack fidgeting, she asked, "Do you always come to the funerals of your victims?"

"Often, I do."

"I wonder how much Josephine's worth now?"

"A lot more after her husband's death."

As they whispered to one another, she knew she was in trouble. He was handsome, intelligent and good company. She'd not told him too much about herself but somehow it felt like he knew who she was without her needing to say anything.

He lifted the side of her hat so he could better see her face. "Do you want to take the hat off now?"

"Men's hats come off indoors, whereas women's hats stay on."

"Ah, forgive me. I didn't realize the protocol. Thanks for the etiquette lesson."

She adjusted the brim of her hat. "It stays on all the time. By the way, nice suit."

"Thank you. It's my funeral suit."

The slightest giggle escaped her lips. "It's nice." She looked at the front. "Where's the coffin?"

"Not here yet but it looks …" He looked back at the door. "Yep. Here it comes."

She turned to see eight men carrying the coffin on their shoulders. They placed the coffin on the stand at the front and immediately a young woman, who appeared to work for the funeral home, tried to place a large arrangement of white lilies on the top of the coffin. Gizelle stood up to help her.

Once they were seated, a robed minister with a white collar stood and moved to the microphone. Organ music sounded and he gave an upward wave of his hands as the signal for everyone to stand. The words of the hymn were printed on the booklet they'd been given at the door, but with her upbringing Gretel knew it by heart.

She kept her mouth clamped closed, refusing to sing the words that brought back memories of a painful childhood. Everyone sat when the song was over and the minister said some kind words about Glen Welch, a regular member of his church. As he droned on, Gretel's mind switched off Glen Welch and onto Ryan Castle. More than anything she wanted him caught red-handed with the diamonds and then thrown in jail. She wanted him to suffer like he'd caused her to suffer.

Gretel closed her eyes wanting to be anywhere other than at a funeral.

She'd spent most of her younger years in churches

and she'd had enough. She glanced over at Jack ready to make some excuse about a headache, but quickly changed her mind when she heard Gizelle being called up to say a few words.

Gizelle said how grateful she was that Glen had stepped in to raise her after her own father died in an accident when she was two. Her only regret was that she didn't spend more time with Glen. When Gizelle finished telling lies, it was Glen's brother, Reginald's, turn. It wasn't long before he had everyone laughing about the antics he and Glen got up to when they were younger. Even Gretel had trouble keeping a straight face and at one point a giggle escaped.

After a prayer, another hymn was sung. The coffin was again lifted up and borne outside by the pallbearers.

Since there was no one sitting between Gretel and the door, she got up and hurried outside and away from the doorway while she waited for Jack. After half the crowd had come out, Jack joined her.

"That was a quick getaway," he said.

"I didn't want anyone to see me."

"With that hat, it won't be a problem."

She knew he was disappointed in her, and for her that was familiar territory thanks to hearing—constantly—from her parents what a dreadful person she was. Even though she'd not seen them for many years, the hurts were still ingrained.

"The graveyard's half an hour away."

"You mean we're going to the grave to watch him …"

"Yes. And just act normal. You seem jumpy and twitchy. Eyes and ears open. That's what's needed."

"Well, I'm not used to being—"

"You're not used to being out in the daylight in your line of business."

She couldn't help smiling. "*Former* 'line of business,' and that's not so. Most of my decorating clients see me during the day."

He made no further comment as they walked up the road.

As Gretel and Jack walked over to the grave, Gretel said, "I've always found graveyards so peaceful. I don't think they're scary at all. They might be at night. I suppose under a full moon I'd be nervous if I was here alone, but during the day there's such a sense of tranquility. Don't you think so?"

"Not particularly. I think there's sadness and sorrow all around. People have lost loved ones."

"It's the cycle of life. We live and then we die, so we'd better have a good time in the middle."

"You don't believe in the hereafter, Ms. Koch, daughter of Brady Koch the famous evangelist?"

She didn't like to be associated with her family. Many times she'd considered legally changing her name, but more often than not she'd had different names every few months. "I did believe and then I didn't. Now I don't. What about you?"

"I don't know." He scratched behind his ear. "I keep changing my mind about the whole thing."

"My father would say just because you change your mind, doesn't change what's going to happen after you die." She stifled a laugh. She knew her father's standard answers to all the usual objections.

"Ah, ministers, they do like to put the fear into you."

"Ain't that the truth?"

They smiled at one another. At least they could agree on that. Now that they were getting closer to the other people, Gretel kept her head down and stayed that way until the coffin was lowered into the grave.

People were gathered around the open grave in a circular formation. When the minister said a prayer, Gretel looked up at the crowd, scanning the sea of faces. Then she spotted her silver-haired lawyer, Cameron Wiltshire, looking ever so good in his dark suit. Who knew an older man could look that good? Most of the guests appeared to be lawyers so she wasn't surprised to see him there. Then her gaze was pulled to the man standing next to Cameron.

The prayer was still going on and everyone else had their eyes closed and heads bowed except for Gretel and the man staring right back at her. He was heavily tanned with ice blue eyes and short dark hair. Did he know Cameron? Somehow he didn't look like a lawyer —he looked like he spent all his time in the sun at resorts to get that tan. His suit was expensive and he had a chunky watch on his wrist, barely showing under his cuff. She had no interest in watches, but something told her this one was designer.

She stared back at him refusing to be intimidated by the chill in his gaze.

Did he recognize her from the newspapers?

Or … could he be the man who was in the Welches' house that night? The one who tried to pull her off the hedge?

He was roughly the same height and build, she remembered.

Her blood ran cold.

The thought of that made her break eye contact and lower her head.

Looking back up to memorize his face, she was stunned. He was gone.

CHAPTER 12

SHE HAD TO FIND HIM, and to do that she had to move away from Jack. "Excuse me," she whispered and then took a step backward and bumped into someone. "I'm sorry," she said to the middle-aged woman whose foot she'd stepped on. The woman gave no reply, merely scowled at her and grabbed the top of her leg.

Gretel wove her way through the people and stood at the back of the crowd. She spotted him in the distance about to get into a car. As Gretel hurried toward him, she took out her cell phone, held it up and took a couple of snaps. He zoomed away and she ran the best she could in her five-inch heels to the road and snapped the plate number.

Then he was gone.

She turned around and saw the crowd dispersing and Jack marching toward her. What would she say to him about leaving so suddenly? She couldn't tell him she had a feeling that this guy was the man she'd bumped into when she went back to rob the Welches' house.

"Where did you go running off to?" he asked.

"I saw someone I thought I knew from school. Then he took off fairly quickly. I'm not sure why. Did you see the man that left?"

"No. I didn't notice anyone leave except you. Old boyfriend was it?"

"Of course not. You think everyone's my boyfriend."

He grinned. "You can't deny that I've been right fifty percent of the time."

"Past tense. And only one man you know of has been my *ex*-boyfriend—Ryan Castle."

"I'm going to talk with Josephine. Do you want to come along?"

She shook her head. The woman knew her parents. "I can't think of anything worse."

He blew out a deep breath as though she was frustrating him. Then he reached into his jacket pocket and took out his car keys. "Here." He held them out to her. "Keep out of trouble." He plonked them into the palm of her hand.

"I'll try." Walking off toward his parked car, she was pleased the funeral was over. It hadn't been too bad, as funerals went. At least she'd spent the day with Jack, which she was enjoying more and more.

As soon as she was settled in the car, she emailed the photos of the man and the car to herself. In the description, she wrote a 'note-to-self' to find out who the man was and ID the car. Kent monitored her email and he'd see it and know what she meant. If they ever took her computer from her, there would be no emails to trace to Kent.

Her own lawyer hadn't recognized her, or he would've said hello. What if he knew something helpful about the case? She made a mental note to ask him.

Seeing no one was anywhere near the car, she opened the glove box and looked through it. She'd half expected to see a gun, but all she found was paperwork to do with the car along with a receipt for a car service. Address? She'd always wondered where he lived but nothing there told her that information.

To kill time, she had a better look at the photos she'd taken. It seemed a complete waste of time. She only got the back of him and one fuzzy frame of him driving away. The plate number too was out of focus. Still, if anyone could make something of it, it'd be Kent.

Looking up, she saw Jack coming toward her talking with Josephine's brother-in-law—the lawyer. If she didn't know better she would've thought they were friends. But wasn't he an enemy? He'd certainly stopped Josephine from answering a lot of their questions.

The lawyer got in his car and Jack continued on toward her. As soon as he slid in beside her, she said, "Please tell me we're not going to the wake."

"Free alcohol, and ritzy food? Are you going to pass it up?"

"Yes. I'm not a drinker."

He smiled. "No, we're not going. The wake is for the friends and family. I think we can give that a miss, don't you?"

"Most definitely." She took off her hat.

"Finally." He stared at her. "Blonde suits you, but not as much as your natural dark hair."

"Thanks. I think."

"I'll take you home. You can have the rest of the day to yourself." He looked over at her and grinned.

Gretel was more than a little disappointed that he didn't offer to take her out to dinner or at least coffee so they could debrief about the day's events. They'd been getting on so well. It was a letdown.

When she opened the door of her apartment feeling no better, she took off her wig, and tossed it and the large hat and coat on the coffee table. Then she flopped down on the couch. The day had been a complete waste. They'd learned nothing about the Welch case nor anything more about the Welch family. Although, it wouldn't be a waste if Kent was able to ID the man who'd been staring at her.

As far as Ryan was concerned, she didn't see Jack doing anything to locate him. He kept saying he had people on it, but who were these people? Were there any people or was he just saying that to keep her on his side?

As she lay there looking up at the ceiling, she remembered going to a lake cabin with Ryan one night. He'd referred to it as his parents' lake house. It was a few hours' drive away. He drove there in the dark and they had stayed two nights. She had no idea of the address, but she was pretty sure she could drive there.

Gretel bolted upright. What if he was hiding-out there? She pulled up maps on Google Earth and tried to find her way by following the roads. That led her to Lake George. She'd never heard him mention the name of the place. Maybe he thought she wouldn't remember where it was.

She raced to a cell phone and called Kent. "Two things. Firstly, were you able to get an ID on the man or the car from today?"

"Nope. Still working on it."

"The other thing is, I need you to see if anyone by the last name of Castle owns anything in Lake George."

"Give me one minute." She heard him tapping keys. "Nope. Nothing."

She looked back at her computer screen. "Are you sure?"

"Yes. Why?"

She told him the story. "I'm pretty sure I have the exact location of it on Google Earth. I'm looking at it on the computer screen now."

"Give me an address."

Gretel zoomed in closer and gave him the address.

"That is owned by a company."

"Are you sure?"

"Of course." He gave her the name.

"Means nothing to me, not familiar at all."

"I can find out who the owner or owners are."

"Yes please." Then she heard him yell. "What's wrong?"

"Power's just gone out. Give me a minute; my back-up's not working either on the computer or the Internet. If I can't fix it, I'll have to start the generator."

"Oh, a generator." She thought they only had those out in the country. "Fine. Call me when—"

She heard a loud click and then nothing.

Now she had something tangible, but how would she get there without Jack knowing? Or better yet, take him with her. She'd talk with Jack about this first thing tomorrow.

CHAPTER 13

Gretel was still in bed the next morning when she heard the knock at the door.

"What now?" She grabbed her robe and answered the door while she was still tying it in the middle.

It was Jack. She kind of thought it might be.

He looked her up and down. "Did I wake you?"

"I was awake."

He breezed through the open door as if he owned the place.

"What time is it?"

"Seven."

"Seven!"

"Yes. I got a call last night from Doug Greeves. He wants to tell us something."

She rubbed her head, still fuzzy-brained and in much need of coffee. "Remind me who he is again?"

"The lawyer partner of Glen Welch. He'll be at my office at 7:45."

She couldn't recall him at all. "7:45? That's a very precise time."

"He has to work after he talks with us. He's got a lot on his plate now that his partner has gone. He tells me people are leaving his firm left and right."

"How much time do I have before we have to leave?"

"You get dressed, I'll make you a cup of coffee."

"I'll try to hurry." She half turned to go to and then heard him making clanging sounds near her coffee machine. "Do you even know what you're doing?"

"Of course. I can make a cup of coffee. I made you one before."

"I usually don't wake up before nine." She hoped he'd make a note of that.

He folded his arms across his chest. "What time did you wake up when you were incarcerated?"

She got his point and it wasn't just his words. It was the way his deep hazel eyes bore through her. The last thing she wanted was to end up back in the prison-orange jumpsuit. "Give me five minutes."

She headed to her bedroom and closed the door behind her. Then she remembered about finding Ryan Castle's lake house. She'd find the right moment and tell Jack about it. Now, while he was focused on Doug Greeves, it wasn't the right time. She pulled on the first clothes she could find, a simple navy-blue dress with a high neck, short sleeves, and a hemline that ended just above the knees. After she ran a brush through her hair, she applied a lick of makeup. She pushed her feet into sandals and then opened the door. "I'm ready." She had expected to see him in the kitchen with coffee, but he was sitting on the couch. "I'm ready except I do need my coffee."

"We can grab some on the way."

What had he been doing all that time? "What happened to you making coffee for me?"

"I thought it'd take too much time. Easier to get some on the way."

Had he been searching her apartment? She saw her laptop computer on the coffee table. Had he looked in it? There wasn't really anything interesting to see, so that was no real concern. Valuables were hidden in her apartment, but if an official search of her apartment had turned up with zero, she was sure he wouldn't find anything.

She closed the door behind them and headed out of the building with him.

"Did you have someone in your apartment just now?" he asked suddenly.

"No, why?"

"I'm sorry, I just barged in without a second thought."

"It's fine. No one was there. I don't have many friends."

He frowned at her. "You're acting a little odd. I

thought you were worried I'd seen something I shouldn't see."

That statement made her uneasy. He must've known she was hiding *things*, not a person. She laughed to cover up. "It's too early in the morning without coffee and all that. I didn't mean to seem strange, or odd or whatever you said. I guess I am a little different when I'm not allowed to take my time waking from a deep sleep."

He chuckled. "Sorry about that."

After he parked his car near his office, he bought her a take-out coffee. While they were going up in the elevator to his office, she asked, "Do you have any idea what this man is going to say?"

"None. I have no idea, but I'm pretty sure it'll be interesting."

"Can't wait." She took a cautious sip of her coffee. "Mmm, good. Hot."

As soon as they got out of the elevator, someone met them and told them in which room Doug Greeves was waiting.

"You can come in the room too," Jack told her in a way that was a command.

Gretel nodded in agreement. Doug wouldn't know who she was, she hoped. She certainly didn't know him.

When they walked into the room, Gretel stopped and stared. Was this the man with the ice-blue eyes, the guy from the funeral? When she got closer, she saw that it wasn't.

Jack introduced Gretel as his associate, and then they both sat in front of Doug.

"What is it you have to tell us?" Jack asked.

"I suppose by now you know that Glen Welch's firm is in financial difficulties."

"Yes I did hear that. Mind you, I was quite surprised," Jack commented.

"His death hasn't helped us. We're losing more clients. No one wants to be associated with us now, it seems."

"Sorry to hear it." Jack waited for him to say more. The silence continued longer than was comfortable before Doug uttered his next words.

"The bright light is the insurance money he left to the firm in the event of his death. That will pay off our debts, and we can close our doors solvent. It'll be hard for us to walk away, but I think it's best all the partners go their separate ways. Anyway, all that aside, what I need to tell you is that Josephine approached me in a confidential capacity to inquire about a divorce."

"That is interesting."

Gretel asked, "Do you know why she asked you and not another lawyer, one that wasn't connected with her husband or the firm?"

"Because we were friends."

Jack raised his eyebrows. "Friends?"

"No, not like that. Genuine friends."

"What did she say exactly?" Jack asked.

"She just ... she just asked me what she'd get out of it. She knew the firm was in financial trouble and her husband wouldn't stop spending. I had to tell her half of nothing was nothing. She'd probably end up in debt and might have to bankrupt herself. As we all would unless ..."

"Unless?"

"Unless he died first." He looked at Jack. "Before she filed for divorce."

"We're in touch daily with the insurance company and if there's been any wrongdoing there won't be a payout. Naturally they're holding off until the investigation is complete."

"I know. You see, Josephine is in a good solid financial situation thanks to his death, and all this for a woman who was considering divorce." He stared at Jack as though driving his point home.

"I get what you're saying."

Gretel imagined Doug Greeves in a court of law. He was good, but definitely not subtle.

"So you're telling me—all things considered—Josephine makes a pretty good suspect."

Doug nodded.

"I'm sorry, but didn't you say you were a good friend of Josephine's? It's surprising that you're not keeping quiet."

"I take the law seriously." His mouth turned down at the corners and he looked at Jack before he continued, "I can't say whether she knew about the firm's financial problems. I doubt Glen would've told her. He was a high flyer, too used to splashing money around. Me, I'm more careful. I didn't come from money and I know what it is to live without it. I'm not so reckless. All that said, I did my best to convince Josephine to stay with Glen. She thanked me for my thoughts and I never heard anything, but now he's been killed and I have to wonder."

"What is it you're wondering?" Jack asked.

"I don't want to point the finger, but Glen's death solves a lot of problems for Josephine." He sat back and his mouth twitched with a self-satisfied smirk.

"She's not the only one who benefited as you just pointed out," Jack told him.

"That's true, but without Glen, we don't have a firm. I wouldn't have wanted him gone. There's no point continuing the firm. Without him we're just another law firm."

"The money has cleared your debts."

"Yes. Yes, it has done that."

"You think she killed him for the money?" Jack asked point-blank.

"I'd rather not say what I think. I just wanted you to know that she was considering divorce." He glanced at his watch. "I've got a nine o'clock."

"Thanks for coming in." The two men stood and shook hands. When Gretel stood, she didn't offer her hand and he gave her a nod before he walked away.

When he was at the door, Jack said, "Just a minute."

He turned around.

"Where did the conversation take place regarding her asking about divorce?"

"At some fundraiser or other. I can't tell you the date or exactly where the conversation took place. It was months ago. Maybe as much as six months ago."

"Is there anything else you can tell us?"

"No, that's all."

"And did you want out as well? Did you want out of the firm?"

"Never. And he was my friend. That's why I encouraged Josephine to stay with him. That's what he would've wanted. He spent money to keep her happy. That was his focus." He glanced at his wristwatch. "I really should go."

"Thank you for bringing this to our attention. It's helpful to know she was considering getting out of the marriage. We're working with the insurance assessors to get to the truth of the matter."

"Good."

As soon as he left, Gretel stared at Jack. "With friends like him, who needs enemies, right? Why did he tell us all that about Josephine, even if it's true? And how do we know it is true? I'm guessing you asked him about where the conversation took place because you could try to get some surveillance of her going into his office or them meeting somewhere. Convenient he doesn't remember where or when."

"Yes, but she's not likely to make an appointment with him at the same law firm as her husband. She might've been better served to talk to an outside law firm. It doesn't ring true and if he was that good of a friend to Glen, what was to stop him telling Glen his wife was so unhappy?"

"If he did it, what was his motive? Was he in love with Josephine? She seems to like lawyers. Perhaps he wanted out of the partnership. He kills Glen, both Josephine and he get payouts to pay off debts and then they live happily ever after on the millions that the insurance company has to pay out on the stolen jewels. Now he's changed his mind and is throwing her under the bus. Perhaps he's grown tired of her and wants it all to himself. Some men will easily choose money over love." Especially if it's only pretend love, she thought.

"We need him under surveillance." He got up and marched out of the interview room and Gretel followed him to his office.

"Jack, was he the man who was drunk at the Welch house the night of the robbery?"

"No. It wasn't him." Jack chuckled. "I don't think Greeves would lose control so easily. That man is one calculated … person."

Doug Greeves was another crooked lawyer, she knew that much. It oozed from every pore.

Then, she waited for Jack to make some calls before the magical 'right moment' came to mention the lake house.

CHAPTER 14

"I HAVE SOME EXCITING NEWS."

He looked up from his desk. "Somehow, hearing you say that makes me nervous."

"Last night I remembered going to a lake house with Ryan. It wasn't really a lake house it was more of a forest house. And not much of a house, more of a cottage, but he referred to it as his parents' lake house."

When he continued to stare at her blankly, she added, "It's at Lake George."

"You know a place where he might be and you're only mentioning it now?"

"I know. I remembered it last night when I was half asleep. It's the place between awake and asleep when your creative mind is working and your logical mind isn't."

"It's called a hypnagogic state of consciousness."

"Are you sure?"

He gave a nod.

"Why the heck would you know that?"

He shrugged a shoulder.

"It's at Lake George. I followed it on the map, and I have the address." She fished it out of her bag and handed it to him. "It's only a few hour's drive."

"What are you proposing?"

She didn't see why he wasn't reacting to this more positively. Didn't he want to catch Ryan and find the diamonds? "He could be hiding out there."

He breathed in slowly as he pressed his lips together. "He left the hospital, yes. Was he under arrest at the time? No. Did he get a pardon for his crimes for turning you over? Yes."

Gretel leaned forward, "Does he have the stolen diamonds? Yes. Is he a dangerous psychopath? Yes. Should he be off the streets? Yes."

"What do you want me to do, Gretel?"

"Did you lie to me when you said you had people looking for him?"

"No. I didn't. Sit down."

She lowered herself into a chair.

"I have people looking for him, but it's not a high priority. He's not wanted for anything more than questioning over the shooting at the airport where he was the victim. We still don't know who shot him."

Gretel was shocked. "Wasn't it airport security?"

He shook his head. "No. We know from the footage,

the security guard drew his gun and he was shot too. Two men were shot and we don't know who shot either of them. We didn't find any shell casings so there's not much to go on."

"I didn't know."

Gretel saw colored lights and felt like she was passing out. She inhaled deeply and tried her best to keep it together. "Well, you might find him at the lake house. Do I have to go on my own?"

"That would be a bad idea."

"Then you come with me."

"I don't think I can get away from the agency for that long. Not with the murder investigation. It would take me away for a couple of days and it's not possible at the moment."

"It's important. It'll clear my name."

He chuckled. "Your name will never be clear."

"I've never been convicted of anything." She'd never admitted to anything. Not even the last robbery where Ryan took the diamonds. "I want to show you I'm not lying about those diamonds and I want you to know that when he turned me in and said I had them, he really had them. Do you see why this is so bothersome to me? Why isn't this a higher priority?"

When he opened his mouth to speak, she knew he wasn't interested.

She stood, a hand held out to silence him. "I'll go there myself. I'll see you when I get back." She walked out of his office risking her newfound position. Right now making Ryan suffer was like a red flag that she had to follow. Why should he be out there somewhere free, enjoying the fruits of her labor?

The elevator door was open, and she slipped into it and closed the doors. She saw Jack was trying to catch up to her, but she didn't care. Maybe things would be different if she had official assurances, but she had nothing on paper. She was so angry she was prepared to suffer as long as Ryan did too.

When the elevator doors opened, an out-of-breath Jack was waiting. "Wait at the café next door. I'll be there in fifteen and then we'll talk, okay?"

With him looming over her, she had to agree. "Okay."

"Good. Calm down, okay?"

She nodded, and then he moved past her and strode into the elevator.

Gretel headed to the café. Something told her she didn't need any more caffeine today so she sat down with a decaf soda.

When Jack finally came in, he ordered a coffee and then sat in front of her. "There are some things I need to go over with you."

"Yes?"

"A decision has been made to seize all your properties and freeze your bank accounts."

She wasn't shocked. She'd thought this was coming. Fortunately, she had overseas bank accounts that they knew nothing about, but if she couldn't leave the country, she had no way of accessing them. "What will I live off? Those rental properties bring me income, and where am I supposed to live?"

"They're allowing you to keep your apartment—your primary place of residence."

She blew out a long breath, grateful to still have her apartment.

"Understand that you got those properties by ill-gotten gains, and by forfeiting them that appeases the countries who want to extradite you."

"Oh, so I'm forfeiting them … willingly?"

He nodded.

"Is that the only way?" She'd need to talk to her lawyer. It sounded like that would be making an admission.

The waitress brought his coffee over. "It's the easiest and best way. You'll still live a comfortable life."

"I will? How am I supposed to pay my bills?"

"Consulting fees."

"You honestly want me to forfeit my properties?" She had five rental properties in New York.

"You need to meet us halfway."

She sucked on her straw. This was never mentioned when the verbal agreement had been made. Would they keep changing the height of the bar? Still, she was out of prison and Jack did seem to be on her side. "Okay, I'll do it to show I'm making amends, meeting you halfway and … avoiding extradition."

"You'll be paid for what you do. It'll be enough to keep up with your expenses on your apartment."

She hoped he wasn't talking about her fake interior design business. "I'll be paid?"

"Yes."

Gretel put her hands on her forehead. "I need a moment to process."

"While you're processing, I've decided that we're taking a trip to Lake George."

She looked up at him. "You mean it?"

He nodded. "What do you know about this lake house?"

"I hope that's where he's holing up. I hope he forgot that we went there. Thanks so much. I don't know why I'm not thinking straight at the moment. I should've thought about this before." Gretel blew out a deep breath.

"You've got a lot going on." Jack offered a sympathetic smile.

"Yes, too much. I've looked up all the holiday and permanent rental listings at Lake George—"

"Please tell me it's vacant."

Gretel nodded. "As far as I know it is. It's never been listed anywhere. At least not through the Internet. I checked."

"Good."

"Convenient." Gretel smiled, pleased with herself for gathering that information.

"I know you're fully focused on Ryan Castle, but I've

also got to get answers about who killed Glen Welch. Surely with your connections you can find out what became of the jewelry? It would go a long way to keeping you from going back to prison if you're useful to us on this one."

"Wait a moment. I'm not giving up anything if there's a chance I'll be going back to prison."

He shook his head. "You won't. I just meant that we'd be very grateful and the higher-ups will see that they've made the right choice."

"I see what you mean. I've asked around and no one has seen or heard of this jewelry being offered up for sale anyway. That in itself is extremely suspicious. I've always thought it was an inside job and I'm still sure. There. Isn't that helping?"

He stared into her eyes and she felt him probing into her mind, searching the dark recesses. "Yes, that is a help. It's not following the usual pattern of robberies if your contacts have heard nothing."

"The wife had everything to gain, but then again she was away at the time. Glen's business partner was quick to point the finger at her. Gizelle, Glen's step-daughter, would've also gained since the mother had gained. Or the three of them could've been in it together." She shook her head. "I don't know about motives and why people murder other people. I've never liked violence." She thought back to the empty base of that safe. She hadn't put it back together and no one had mentioned that, but she had locked it behind her, so maybe they hadn't noticed how she'd left it. Unless Jack knew of it and was keeping it from her. "Do you know anything about this that you haven't said?"

"You know everything that I know."

"Ah, good." Hopefully that meant he didn't know she'd been back at the house. "I wonder if Ryan's got the diamonds stashed at the lake house. He could've buried them out there somewhere."

"That's not likely, is it? He's taken you there, so he knows you know where it is."

"It's a long shot I suppose. When are we going there?"

"Today." He took a mouthful of coffee.

"Really?"

"Yes. Going up there with you will mean putting Glen Welch's case on the back burner. I'll have to do some delegating. Go home and get ready. Give me an hour and I'll stop by and get you." He drained the last mouthful of coffee and left her there.

When she got home, she called Kent and it went to message. She ended the call. Then she emailed her sister's unused email account knowing Kent would see it, stating where she was going, and what time she expected to be back.

Gretel hadn't hesitated for a moment when Jack told her to go home. As soon as she had sent the email, she pulled on jeans and a blouse and exchanged her high heels for boots. She also packed some things in her roomy quilted Channel handbag in case they were there longer than expected.

Then she sat waiting on her wide windowsill chewing her fingernails and wondering if she should call her lawyer, Cameron. He hadn't been much use and she hadn't spoken to him since she'd told him about the deal she'd been offered. He'd told her to grab it with both hands, but she could've worked that much out for herself without his exorbitant fee involved. But since the Welch case was all about lawyers, she figured he might have something useful to contribute.

He answered his cell phone with, "Gretel, I was just about to call you."

"You were?"

"Yes. The bank rejected your payment for our fees. I thought you'd prefer a personal call from me rather than have one of my office staff contact you."

"Do you take cash?"

"That's a little unusual, but of course we do, and bitcoin."

"I'm all out of those, but I can bring cash within the next few days."

"Thank you."

"The reason I'm calling is that I'm wondering if you knew Glen Welch very well."

"I knew him. He wasn't in my circle of friends."

"What about his business partner?"

"I know him about the same as Glen Welch. How's it coming along with helping the FBI?"

"It's okay. I'm helping them with the Welch case, and I thought you might know something useful."

"Like what? Are you talking about the Welches' marriage breakdown?"

"Oh. I didn't know it was common knowledge."

"There was talk at the club and that's all I can say. Mind you, there's always talk at the country club."

"What was the talk?"

"They were never there together. Not for the last two years."

Gretel didn't see that as unusual. Many couples went their separate ways and followed their own interests. "Is that all?"

"Yes. That's all I recall. Sorry I can't help you more."

"If you think of anything that might help will you let me know?"

"Are you thinking Josephine had a hand in his death? I heard he was killed in the process of a robbery."

"I'm just trying to gather facts." She smiled when she realized she was starting to sound like Jack. "I'll be out of town for a couple of days and then I'll bring in that payment."

"Look after yourself, Gretel."

"I will." She ended the call then looked down at the traffic going by. It seemed the credit card she used for payments had been frozen. Right at that moment, she didn't care. Today she was free. She wasn't in jail, afraid for her life, with her identity stripped from her. She was Gretel Koch, reformed jewel thief, helping the FBI and she felt good about that. If she could quell the urge to steal, her life might run smoothly.

Her cell phone sounded. She looked down in the street to see if she could see Jack's car. It wasn't there. Turning her attention to her cell phone she saw it was a 'no caller ID.'

"Yes?" she answered with caution.

"Don't try to find me." The call ended.

It was Ryan Castle.

CHAPTER 15

GRETEL'S HEARTBEAT QUICKENED. She opened her mouth to speak, but the call had ended before she could utter a word. Standing up, she tossed the cell phone on the window's ledge.

Did he know that they were heading to the lake house? Did he have someone on the inside at the FBI? Or was it a coincidence? She picked up the phone again and called Jack.

He answered immediately.

"Jack, Ryan Castle. He just called my cell phone."

"What did he want?"

"He said not to come looking for him and then he hung up. Do you have my number monitored?" She was pretty certain they did.

"I don't but I'll get that organized right away in case he calls again. Did he say anything else?"

"That's all he said. Not even his name. His number didn't come up on my phone."

"Stay calm."

"I'll try." She took a deep breath.

"I'm nearly at your place. I'll be there in five."

That made her feel much better. "Okay. I'll be waiting." She ended the call and walked into the kitchen and poured herself a glass of water. Colored lights flickered around her and she felt lightheaded. A few slow, deep breaths and the feeling lessened. She took a couple of headache pills as prevention, washed down by a tall glass of water.

After a moment, she gathered her things together and headed downstairs. She walked out of the building just as she saw Jack's car rolling to a stop. He double-parked, holding up the traffic, and she got in to the sound of beeping horns.

"How are you feeling?" he asked as he drove on.

"I'm okay."

"You don't look it."

"I wasn't expecting to hear from him. Could he know we're going to the lake house? I didn't tell anyone—did you?"

"No. I haven't told anyone other than the people who need to know my whereabouts. There's no way he could've found out."

"Now we know he's not lying in a ditch somewhere, dead from his gunshot wound."

"In a few hours, we should know more about the

call. I've got people working on it. We won't be able to pinpoint where the call originated but we will know whether it came from within the country."

"That'll be something at least." Jack had already assured her Ryan hadn't left the country, so him trying to have the call traced was useless if they could only say whether he was in the country or not.

"Are you sure it was him?" he asked.

"Yes. I know his voice well." She let out a long, drawn-out sigh.

He glanced over at her. "How did it make you feel hearing his voice again?"

"Sick and unnerved." She turned to look at him. "Are you a psychiatrist now?"

He chuckled. "He was your significant other."

"Don't remind me. I have no feelings for him now other than contempt. Don't forget he left me to die in the sinking car when he took off with the diamonds. I still have nightmares about it. The reason I don't like to swim is I don't like the feel of my head being underwater. It gives me claustrophobia. He knew that."

"Then he told us *you* were the one who hid the diamonds."

"Do you believe me now?"

"I do. I believe you, otherwise we wouldn't have offered you the deal. It was the prosecution who swallowed his story. They are the ones who did the deal with him, it wasn't us."

She rubbed her head. "Thank you for believing me."

SAMANTHA PRICE

She felt a little guilty for keeping things from him, but self-preservation was the key to her survival. If she didn't look after herself who would? The headache tablets were making her drowsy, so she put her head back onto the headrest and allowed her heavy eyelids to close.

"What beautiful countryside."

She was jolted awake and saw they were out of the city and very much in the country. "How long was I asleep?"

"Long enough for me to hear three different kinds of snoring."

She put a hand over her face. "Really? I was snoring?"

"Only in the most polite way."

She pushed herself up into the seat. "That's dreadful. I'm sorry."

He took a deep breath. "I should do this more often. I need to take more breaks."

"It's not a vacation, though. It's work."

"Allow me a moment to pretend I'm off to have a weekend of R&R. Even when I take vacations they aren't really vacations. I'm always thinking about the job. More often than not, I'm called back in. There's no real time that's 'off duty.'"

"It's not so much a job then, it's a lifestyle."

"You got it."

"Do you enjoy it?"

"I do. I like fitting the pieces together and there's no

greater sense of satisfaction than a job well done and getting a bad guy off the streets at the same time." He glanced over at her. "Or a bad gal."

"That's okay. I took guy to include females. Like when the Bible says man, it often refers to man and woman, but not always." She smoothed down her hair. "So, you don't take time off until you wrap up a case?"

"If the case demands it I don't."

"That can't be good for you."

"That's just the way things are. Life's never perfect. We humans are always striving for something. When we reach one goal, there's always another one that captures our attention."

She knew what he meant. Over the last few years she'd done about fifteen 'last' jobs. It wasn't that she needed the money, and she knew each time she stole there was the risk of getting caught. There was nothing so enticing as a new job, though, and no words to describe the euphoria that came when she found out she'd gotten away with it. "That was my last job, the one that I did where Ryan Castle played a part. *Only* job if anyone wants to know. The only one I'm officially admitting to."

"Did you enjoy stealing? You must have plenty of money by now."

"I don't want to talk about it, if that's okay. It's all in the past."

"Fair enough."

"I was caught because I trusted someone."

"Yes, that was a bad decision." He seemed amused. "The man you loved double-crossed you."

She had to agree, but did he have to rub it in? "Enough about me. Are you married?" She glanced at his finger—no wedding ring, as she'd already noted. "I see you don't wear a ring. And your wife would have to be pretty understanding since you're never home."

"Never been married."

She waited for more, but nothing came. "No long story to entertain me? Why has no woman ever trapped you in her web? Come on, you know everything about me, and I know nothing about you."

He glanced over at her. "I very much doubt I know everything about you." He looked at the car's dashboard. "According to the GPS it's only five miles away."

"Get your gun ready."

"Always is."

Two miles further along, he turned up a dirt track. "It's rough, and they had rain a few hours ago which would've washed away any tracks."

When the cabin finally came into view, there was no sign of life and no car in sight.

"I'll knock. You stay in the car. I'll leave the keys in the ignition. There's a gun in the glove box, but it's strictly for emergencies."

"I don't know how to use it."

"Remind me to show you. It's a good skill to have, just in case."

When he was halfway to the house, she scooted

over into the driver's seat and then leaned back to the passenger side and carefully took the gun out of the glove box. It was heavier than she thought it would be. After she turned it over and had a good look at it, she placed it on the seat beside her in case she needed it.

From the car, Gretel watched Jack knock on the door and when there was no answer, he moved to look in the windows. He walked around the back and when he was out of sight, she became nervous. What if he was shot and they came after her? She looked down at the gun. Did she just need to pull the trigger or was there some kind of lock on it? It might be better if she drove away, but no, she couldn't leave Jack alone unless he'd been killed. She shook her head hoping none of what she'd thought about would happen. This place was giving her the chills.

A few minutes later he was back. "Are you sure this is the right place?"

She opened the car door and got out. "Yes. This is it. Should we go in?"

"Not yet. We have to wait for the warrant."

"What warrant?" She stared at Jack. Surprises of any kind weren't good.

CHAPTER 16

"Didn't I mention it?"

"You said nothing about a warrant." She had thought it was going to be just the two of them and if a warrant was coming from somewhere, someone had to be bringing it.

"I've got the local police coming soon and I had the email I got earlier today from Judge Wryner emailed to them."

"Oh, I didn't realize."

He took a step closer. "Gretel, if we don't do things by the book there's no point. If we find the diamonds on the premises and we have no warrant it won't go down well in court. It won't count if it's unlawful entry. In my career I've seen too many criminals walk because of improper procedure."

"Got it." She nodded. "I don't think of all those things. I just want him to be found with the diamonds." In her mind, things had played out differently. She'd brought her lock picking tools and then she thought she'd break in after they'd argued about it, that he'd finally agree to her picking the lock, and then they'd search every inch of the place. "How long will they take to get here?"

He glanced at his watch. "They should be here any time now."

Just then they heard cars. A police car appeared through the trees, followed by another one.

Jack walked over to meet them when they pulled up. They introduced themselves while Gretel stood back. Then the uniformed officers moved ahead of him and knocked on the door again. They yelled out, and then they entered the premises by kicking down the door.

When the four police officers walked into the house, Jack turned to Gretel. "Are you coming?"

"Sure." She walked past the broken lock. If they'd asked her, she could've got them in without destroying anything, but that clearly wasn't the way they did things. There was a faint smell of smoke and she walked over to the fireplace. "There's been a fire here recently."

"Strange ... it's not cold enough yet for that," said Jack.

"It gets cold at night, and the fire might not have been for keeping him warm. He might have been burning something. Documents, evidence, who knows?"

"True. They'll collect the ashes and have them sent for testing."

She walked to the kitchen, opened the fridge and picked up a partly-consumed carton of milk. "Two days until its use-by date." He always had milk in his coffee. "Someone has been here recently. What if he's just gone out somewhere and he's coming back?"

"He'll get a big surprise. I wonder if the diamonds are stashed in here somewhere or buried outside like you suggested?" He walked closer to her. "I'll have them look around and see if there's any sign of anything being freshly dug."

"Can I look around out there now?"

He nodded. "It wouldn't hurt."

She walked out of the cabin and unease skittered down her spine. Was she being watched? She looked around. Nothing could be seen beyond the cabin but trees. She walked around the house looking for suitable areas where he could've buried the diamonds. The trouble with hunting for diamonds was that they were so small—they could've been hidden anywhere. Even still in the cabin, in the walls or hidden in hollowed out furniture. It was impossible to search every inch.

After twenty minutes looking around the outside area, she gave up. It was like looking for a needle in a haystack. She headed back to the cabin. Jack was talking to one of the officers beside their cars. Then they looked back at the house and from Jack's hand movements, she knew he was asking them to do a search of the surrounding area.

She waited by the house for Jack. When the police were gone, Jack walked over to her. "They came up with nothing."

"I guessed that. He's left nothing here. No clothing. The only sign he's been here is the milk."

"And the recent fire."

"Can I have one more look inside?"

"Sure."

Back inside, she walked around the kitchen examining the cabinetry for odd-looking joins. Then she moved to the bathroom and did the same. Lastly, she checked the furniture. There was nothing anywhere to indicate anything hidden. There were the walls, but she couldn't really take to them with a sledgehammer. That went beyond the scope of a search warrant.

She flung herself down on the couch, defeated. "I was hoping he'd be here, and I would find him and the diamonds."

Jack leaned against the living room wall. "I'm sorry it didn't work out. Sometimes life—"

"Please don't give me any speeches. I've had enough of those from my family to last a lifetime."

He chuckled. "What about friends or relatives of Ryan?"

She sighed. "I never met any of them. He said his parents once owned this place. He told me they're both dead, but any or all of that could be a lie."

"That's right." He folded his arms across his chest. "Do you mean to tell me you didn't know?"

"Didn't know what?"

"This place is in a company name which we eventually traced to him."

"Okay." She stared at him wondering what point he was making.

"You didn't know who Ryan Castle's father was?"

She shrugged. "Mr. Castle I presume?"

"No, it wasn't, and Ryan Castle is not *his* real name." He kept staring at her. "All the way up here I was waiting for you to say something. I can't believe you don't know."

"Tell me!"

"Ryan's father was Earl Butterworth."

Her mouth fell open. Josephine Welch's first husband was Earl Butterworth. Ryan was involved in the case they were working on.

CHAPTER 17

GRETEL'S HEADACHE came back with a vengeance. She put her hand to her forehead. Kent should've been the one to tell her that Castle wasn't Ryan's real name. That was the kind of information she paid him for. She dropped her hands into her lap and looked up at Jack. "Who is his father?" she asked hoping to get a different answer.

"None other than Earl Butterworth."

"Earl Butterworth is Josephine's first husband. So Earl was married to someone before Josephine and they had Ryan?"

"Correct."

"So Ryan's stepmother is Josephine?"

He nodded.

"I never knew."

"He was in boarding school for much of his life, didn't even come home for the holidays."

"That was not nice."

"You had no idea?"

"No. Why didn't you tell me? When did you find all this out?"

"Earlier today when we were organizing the search warrant."

Gretel sighed, looking at the floorboards. "The two cases are linked. You thought you were working on two and now it's kind of one. I had no idea," she repeated. "I didn't even know that Castle wasn't his real name. He had me completely fooled."

"Gretel, I have to ask you this."

"Ask me anything." She held her breath hoping he wasn't going to outright ask if she'd been back to the Welch mansion to look in the safe.

"Is there anything about the case or Ryan Castle that you're holding back?"

Slowly, she shook her head. "Nothing."

"Good." His serious face relaxed slightly. "I was hoping you'd say that."

Their eyes locked and she wondered if he believed her. Did he think she'd say so if she was keeping something from him? There was no way she could tell him about going back to the Welch house that night to steal and seeing another man who might've also been there to steal.

Then they heard cars. He hurried to the window. "We've got company." He drew a gun out of his back pocket.

"Who is it?" She jumped off the couch and peered out the window to see two large 4x4 vehicles.

Men poured out of the vehicles and they all had big guns. Ryan had sent people there to kill them, she was certain of it.

"Let's go." He pulled on her arm and they ran out the back door and into the trees. He then called for backup.

They heard one of the men yelling. "They're on the run."

They were going to be hunted down like prey and then killed. The men knew they were there because Jack's car was parked outside. After they'd been running for several minutes, working their way up a rise, they stopped and turned around. They couldn't see anyone after them.

"Who are they?" she asked, trying to catch her breath.

"Colombians, by the looks," he whispered. "I wouldn't mind betting this has something to do with drugs. Come on, we've got to keep on the move."

Drugs and diamonds? They turned and kept running. "Where are we going?"

"Anywhere. We're going up the hill so we can see them if they come after us." After a while they stopped again and looked back. "Can you see anything?"

"No."

"We need to keep going."

"What if they're not following us?"

"I'm not willing to take that risk."

"The police are coming, aren't they?"

"Hopefully."

A bullet sounded and he pushed her to the ground. She was still alive; she looked over at him to see his shoulder bleeding. "You've been hit."

He looked down, holding his arm and gritting his teeth. Then he jumped up and pulled her to her feet. "GO!"

She was too scared to leave, but he started running and she had to follow. "Aren't you going to shoot back?"

"Not until I get a clear shot."

A bullet zinged past them again. This was too real.

"That was close," he said pulling on her arm and running even faster. He stopped when he saw some discarded building materials. Then he pulled her behind some corrugated iron that was wedged between a clump of trees. "I see him," Jack said right before he took aim and fired.

Another shot was fired at them and bored straight through the iron right beside her. It sent their make-shift barrier flying. Jack pushed her to the ground and covered her with his body.

Police sirens sounded in the distance.

Would they arrive when it was too late?

"Stay still." Jack raised himself up. "They're leaving."

"Are you sure?"

"They're heading back to the cabin. I've got eyes on two of them." He pulled out his cell phone. "No service."

Gretel sat up and saw his blood-soaked shoulder. "You've got to get to a hospital." He stood up, tore off his shirt, ripped it into strips and gave her a section. "Wrap this around the wound. It just needs pressure to stop the bleeding."

She took her eyes off his abs long enough to bandage his shoulder.

Shots rang out again and he pushed her back to the ground and covered her with his body. Her face was pressing against the earth. She closed her eyes tightly.

It sounded like there was a shootout back at the cottage. After a while, the shooting subsided, and they sat up.

"What if they've shot all the police?"

"Then more would be on their way and they'd know that. I'm sure that's the end of it."

Gretel hoped he was right.

"You stay here and hide the best you can. I'll go down and take a look."

"I'm coming too."

He turned to face her and put both hands up. "Stay, Gretel."

"No. I'll come with you."

"You'll need to be prepared to run again."

"I used to run track. I've got good endurance I can run all day, just don't leave me here alone."

He huffed. "Stay close behind me."

When they reached the cabin, they saw the two police cars but the two SUVs were gone.

"I hope they're not waiting for us in the cabin," she whispered.

He turned around to face her. "You stay here." He put his hand in his pocket and pulled out the keys. "If anything happens get the hell out of here."

She grabbed the keys. "Be careful."

He didn't answer her; he walked ten paces and stopped still. Gretel ran up to see what he was staring at. Bodies lay there motionless, lifeless, and cold. Gretel counted them. There were eight. Four of them were the shooters and four were the police.

She covered her mouth as she cried out, and then her legs gave way beneath her.

CHAPTER 18

JACK RUSHED to her side and with an arm around her waist moved her to where she couldn't see the bodies. "Keep calm."

"I'm okay."

"I need to make a call." He pulled out his cell phone and spoke to someone. Gretel didn't even know what was said. Then he sat on the ground with her. "They're two minutes away. Have you seen a dead body before?"

"Once or twice, unfortunately. Were these people after Ryan or us?"

"Ryan I'd guess. They were too late, just like us. Where is Ryan Butterworth headed?" he said as though speaking his thoughts aloud. He stood up and held out his hand. "Sit in the car until the police come. It's much more comfortable."

She grabbed hold of his right hand and stood. "Did you tell them you've been shot?"

"Yes. It's just a flesh wound, I'm sure."

"I don't want to be alone. I'll stay with you. In case you faint or something."

Jack managed a smile.

The sound of the ambulance headed their way was one of the nicest sounds Gretel had heard. Jack and she looked at each other and no words were needed.

Jack's shoulder was tended to while he and Gretel were questioned by some of the same officers who'd been at the house earlier.

The bullet had grazed Jack's shoulder. After his wound was properly dressed, the two of them were driven to the station in separate vehicles to make official statements.

By the time they both finished, it was eight o'clock at night. An officer drove Jack and Gretel back to his car.

By the light of the police car headlights, Gretel saw the vicinity was surrounded by crime scene tape.

"I never want to see this place again," Gretel said as they walked to the car.

"You and me both."

"You can't drive with your shoulder."

"My shoulder won't bother me. I hope you've still got the keys."

"I have and I'm driving." She unlocked the car and got into the driver's seat. After hesitating, he got into the passenger side.

Once they had gone back down the dirt track and she'd turned back onto the road, he said, "I don't think either of us should drive after what's just happened."

"Then what do you suggest?"

"Pull over."

She turned on the blinker and did as he said.

He took out his phone and did a search. "There's a hotel two miles up this road. We can get something to eat and get a decent sleep before we head back."

"That does sound good."

It wasn't long before they had booked side-by-side rooms and were sitting opposite each other at a cozy waterfront restaurant.

As soon as she took a bite of her crumbed fish, she sighed her enjoyment. They'd not eaten anything since that morning. "The police wouldn't tell me anything. Did they know who those men were?"

He shook his head. "No."

"You think they were after Ryan? Maybe they were trying to kill me or you."

"We'll know more if we can identify their bodies."

"Those poor policemen who were killed and their families. It's so tragic."

"I know. One death has a ripple effect. It doesn't just affect the immediate family, and this was four deaths, and the criminals."

"Yes, let's not forget them." Especially not them, Gretel thought. "I feel terrible. If I hadn't asked you to go to the cabin, those men would be alive today. It's hard to believe that one day they were here and now they're gone."

"You can't think like that, Gretel. It is what it is. It's happened and it's in the past. Don't beat yourself up over it. How do you know a worse tragedy mightn't have happened if we didn't come here?"

"I suppose." The phone call from Ryan reverberated around in her head. He'd told her not to look for him. If she'd listened, these men might still be alive.

"As I said, once the criminals are identified, then we'll get a better idea why they were after your boyfriend."

"*Ex*-boyfriend." She looked out over the lake as her stomach clenched. Her well-ordered and organized life was reduced to chaos and uncertainty. She fought back the urge to be sick.

"Are you okay?"

"I can't stop seeing those people lying there each time I close my eyes." She told him what she thought he'd want to hear. Sure, she was concerned about the deaths, but there was nothing that could be done about that now. Truth was, she was more worried about the mess that her life had become.

"It's hard the first time you see something like that."

Gretel appreciated the genuine sympathy he offered her. "Do you think Ryan had something to do with the

Welch robbery?" She now knew it was a strong possibility, what with the family ties.

"He went missing from the hospital the morning after."

"Do we know that for sure?"

"Yes, by all accounts he was still in the hospital, unless he slipped out before they knew it. That's the next road we're about to go down. They raised the alarm that he was missing the morning of the Welch killing, but it is possible he had already left that night."

"Good."

"You say that like you want him to be found guilty."

"I do. I want him to get what's coming to him if he did it."

He leaned forward slightly and stared into her eyes. "It must be awful to find out someone you loved so much deceived you so badly."

"Well, I didn't love him that much. It wasn't Romeo and Juliet or Cleopatra and Mark Antony." She sipped on her straw.

"More like Bonnie and Clyde?"

Her drink spurted out of her mouth. "Oh, gross, I'm sorry." She grabbed a paper napkin and wiped up the mess as she giggled. "Bonnie and Clyde, definitely not. Well, maybe a short-lived version. I should hit you for that, but I might hurt your arm."

He looked down at the bulge that the bandage made underneath his shirt. "Don't hurt me when I'm at my most fragile."

She smiled and then resumed drinking her soda.

THEY'D MADE an early start and had hit the city traffic mid-morning. She'd talked him into letting her drive again. When she was close to her apartment, she said, "I should take you home and then I can collect you in the morning."

"No. I'm okay to drive. It's only a slight graze. Head to your place and I'll take over from there."

"Are you sure?"

"Yes. It's an order."

She smiled. "I can't go against that."

When she pulled up outside her apartment, they both got out of the car.

"Get a good night's rest, Gretel, and I'll check back in with you tomorrow. Let me know if Castle calls you again. Call me anytime, night or day."

"Shouldn't you take a few days off with that shoulder?"

He grinned. "I'll be all right."

She stood and watched him get in the car and drive away.

Gretel was only back in her apartment for an hour when she grew restless.

She couldn't sit around and do nothing.

Ryan's apartment was where she needed to go. Sure

it was a risk, but somehow she felt it was just as much a risk to do nothing. If Ryan had killed Welch, he was a murderer. She'd already had one attempt on her life. Ryan Castle had to be found.

CHAPTER 19

W HEN SHE FOUND a place to park close to Ryan's Brooklyn apartment, she sat there feeling anxious. Then she pulled out a disposable cell phone and called Kent.

"About time," he said as soon as he answered. "Where have you been? I haven't heard a thing from you."

"I went to the lake house. You didn't tell me about the company who owned it, and do you know about Ryan?"

"Yes. I said I'd call you back with info. Next thing I know, there was no answer."

"So you know Ryan's true identity?"

"Yeah," Kent replied, "Ryan Butterworth."

"And you know—"

"His father was Josephine Welch's first husband and Ryan's the only son of Earl Butterworth and

Hilary Butterworth. So he might've stolen the Welches' loot. Seems he lived with the mother after his parents separated, and she shipped him off to boarding school. No love lost there. His father didn't want him when he got the new wife, Josephine."

"I know. Jack told me they never even had him home for the holidays." When there was silence on the other end of the line, Gretel said, "Jack knows—"

"I figured. You're not getting too close to him, are you?"

"Never! I know what I'm doing. He's not going to be interested in someone like me anyway. Have you found out anything else on the Welch family or about Ryan?"

"I'm still searching."

"Good." She ended the call and put her hand on the door of the car, and then hesitated as a sense of danger clouded her mind. Shrugging it off she told herself it was backlash from what had happened at the lake house.

Ryan's apartment was sitting there vacant. It had to hold clues to something. Maybe his relationship with Josephine and Glen Welch, or maybe something to let her know where he could be found. Finally, she pushed the car door open at the same time she pushed aside her reservations.

The police would be keeping an eye on the building in case he headed back there. Surely they wouldn't be on the lookout for a female who might slip into his apartment, would they?

Once she had picked the lock, she would grab the spare key he always kept by the front door. If she had a key—with the fingerprints she'd make sure were on it—no one could call it a break and enter. She hoped not. The fact that she'd been there before meant she didn't have to worry about her prints inside the apartment.

When she got to his apartment, she noticed the door was ajar. She pushed it open. "Is anyone here?"

Silence.

She took another couple steps, enough to see that the entire apartment had been trashed. Furniture was toppled over and things were strewn across the floor. It was one unholy mess.

Gretel made her way through the debris disappointed at the thorough job that had been done. They'd even slashed the upholstery on the couch, and every one of the chairs had been shredded.

When she reached the chaos in the bedroom, Ryan's aftershave hung in the air. Had he been there recently?

Sneaking a peek out the bedroom window, she saw a white car parked on the other side of the street. It had to be the police staking the place out. When she turned her back on the window, she saw his closet.

A memory jumped into her mind. She'd been searching Ryan's hotel room after he'd been shot. As he lay there bleeding on the floor at the airport, he told her the diamonds were hidden in a photo frame. She had wasted no time in grabbing his keys and one of the keys had told her he'd stayed in a hotel so that was where she headed. While she'd been searching his hotel room, someone else came in and she slipped into the closet to hide. There were at least two of them because she heard one call the other by the name Monzo. Were they the Shadows, or were the men at the lake house the Shadows? Or, were they all part of the same group? Or, were there still others out there?

Realizing the people who had ransacked the place could come back, she quickly waded through the mess looking for anything that might give her a clue to Ryan's whereabouts, or the location of the diamonds.

Her eyes were drawn to a photo frame on the bedroom floor. She turned it over and through the shattered glass she saw Ryan and herself with the Eiffel tower behind them. They looked like any other loving couple in their holiday snapshot. It fell from her hands and she stomped on it and squished it into the plush carpet.

After another quick look around, Gretel decided there was nothing left to find, but she was glad she had come. It seemed she wasn't the only one looking for Ryan and the diamonds. If these were the same people who shot at her and Jack, she needed to leave fast.

She headed out of the apartment, leaving the door ajar as she'd found it, and left by the rear door of the building to avoid being seen by the cop in the white car. He'd done a lousy job since he didn't know someone had trashed Ryan's apartment. If he knew, surely Jack would've been informed and Jack would've told her. And there would have been police tape blocking the doorway.

WHEN THERE WAS a break in the traffic, Gretel walked across the street and just as she was nearing the other side, a car sped toward her. She leaped out of the way and then realized the driver was trying to hit her. She sprinted to the sidewalk and the car swerved to follow her, jumping the curb. To avoid getting hit, she ducked into a store. When she was safely inside, she turned for a better look at the car.

The driver was Ryan Castle. She was sure of it. She walked back onto the sidewalk to get a better look. He slammed on the brakes, stuck his head out the window and they locked eyes. He then drove off.

She ran to her car and got in and started it. Then she sped to catch that car. She couldn't let him get away.

When she turned the corner, she spotted his car in the distance. Slamming her foot hard on the gas, she fished her phone out of her bag, and then with one finger got her phone's camera open so she could at least snap the plate number. When she started snapping, he must've seen in the rear-view mirror what she was doing because he started weaving in and out of traffic.

It was no use; she'd never get him now.

Since the FBI was tracking her cell phone, she certainly couldn't call Kent or send him the images from her phone. She pulled her car over to the side and sent the pictures to her own email knowing Kent would see them.

DID RYAN THINK she trashed his apartment, was that why he'd tried to kill her just now? Or was it revenge for what had happened at the lake house? Was Ryan working with those men? If so, he wouldn't be happy that four of them were dead.

ONCE GRETEL WAS HOME, she made herself a cup of coffee and sat down on the couch trying to still her shaking body. Ryan could've run her down and that would've been the end. Jack would've thought it a random hit and run, and Ryan wouldn't have paid for that crime either. The more she thought about it the more she knew he had to get caught and thrown into prison or she'd never be safe.

She abandoned the couch and her coffee to turn on one of her alternate cell phones and call Kent. "Did you get my email?"

"The black vehicle?"

"Yes."

"Registered to one Ryan Castle."

"I knew it. Thanks." She ended the call and picked up her regular cell phone and called Jack.

"Gretel, how are you feeling?"

"Lucky to be alive."

"I know it was a dreadful ordeal."

"I don't mean that. I mean today, just now."

There was silence at the other end of the phone for a moment. "What happened?"

"Ryan Castle tried to run me down."

"In a car?"

"Yes. I happened to be near his apartment …"

"Wait a minute. What were you doing all the way out there?"

"It's not that far."

"I know you were there. You were seen going into his building."

Gretel gritted her teeth. "Okay, I did go into his apartment, but I do have a key. From before. Someone had trashed it before I got there and when I was leaving he tried to run over me when I was crossing the street."

"Are you okay?"

"I'm alive. Unharmed physically, but in the last forty-eight hours I've been shot at and driven at, so … Am I okay mentally? That's a different question. I mean, a different answer."

"Where are you now?"

"At home."

"Sit tight. I'll be there soon."

She slumped back into her couch and sipped her

SAMANTHA PRICE

now lukewarm coffee. It amazed her how quickly love could turn to hate. Had Ryan ever had any feelings for her, or had it all been an act from the start?

Twenty minutes later, there was a knock on her door. A glance at the monitor told her it was Jack. She opened the door and he moved in quickly and closed it behind him. He put a warm hand on her shoulder. "Are you okay?"

"I think so. Just some bruises and a couple of scratches from flinging myself into the doorway of a store. How are you feeling?"

"I'll live."

"I'll show you the photos I took of his car." She grabbed her cell phone and showed him the images she'd snapped.

He held the phone and then his eyebrows knit together. "These are taken from a car?"

"I chased after him."

His mouth fell open. "After he nearly killed you, you chased him?"

"Yes. I had to know if it was him for sure."

"You should *not* risk your life like that. I'll email this to myself and then we can blow up the images."

"I'm sure you'll find the vehicle is registered to him."

"We'll soon find out." He finished emailing the pictures and when his cell phone beeped, he picked it up and tapped on some keys. "Okay, done. We'll hear back soon. Where did this happen?"

"A street parallel to his apartment building."

"Any witnesses?"

"I don't know. I didn't stay and collect names. It was a carpet shop that I ran to."

"Perfect. I'll send someone over to collect CCTV footage and see what we can find."

"Thanks. Do you want coffee?"

"No thanks. It's been a long day. I should go."

She didn't want him to leave, didn't want to be by herself. "What about a calming chamomile tea?"

He grinned. "Okay. I could probably use one of those."

"Have a seat."

As he sat down, he said, "By the way, they weren't able to trace that call."

"When Ryan called me?"

He nodded. "At least we know he's in the vicinity. Until we have him in custody, it might be an idea not to go out alone."

"Does that mean you'll collect me and bring me home every day?"

"Yes."

"Great. It'll be nice to have my own personal body-guard. That'll save on gas too and with the change in my finances I do have to be careful."

When she had placed two mugs of chamomile tea down on the coffee table, she sat next to him. "You must live close by."

"Not too far."

"I'm sensing some unequalness in this relationship. I can't know where you live?"

He picked up his herbal tea and took a cautious sip. "No. It's business, it's not personal."

She felt that was a slap in the face. Wasn't he interested in her at all? Even just a little? "I know that, but when you saved my life it went from business to personal for me. Thank you for saving my life. I haven't thanked you before now. I'm not sure why."

Jack chuckled. "You're welcome, but I was just doing my job."

She'd been right about him not wanting to get involved with someone like her and she couldn't blame him. Jack was more suited to a woman like Monica Blaze. Women like Monica seemed to marry nice men who didn't have a clue what cows they really were. The nice women always got stuck with the abusers.

JACK DIDN'T STAY LONG after his tea. She spent the night alternating between worrying she'd been too forward and flirty with Jack, and worried whether Ryan would try to kill her again.

CHAPTER 20

THE NEXT MORNING, Gretel woke before her alarm and stretched her arms over her head. There was a certain reluctance to move from her bed—one of the few places where she felt safe. Just when she was seriously contemplating spending the day there, her cell phone sounded.

When she looked around for it, she realized it was next to her under the covers. She grabbed it hoping it wasn't Ryan. The caller ID told her it was Jack.

"Hello."

"Be downstairs in twenty."

She had just opened her mouth to tell him she couldn't possibly be ready in that short amount of time. It took her twenty to do her hair, but he'd already ended the call. By now she knew him well enough to know something was up. If she tied her hair back in a ponytail, that could save her time, and if she could persuade him to stop for a takeout coffee that would have to do for breakfast.

She pulled out some clothes—black pants and a cream and black blouse—not knowing if she should be wearing casual or dressy. Hopefully, she'd pass for either in what she had chosen. While she changed her clothes she thought of endless possibilities for the latest developments. They would've found out for certain it was Ryan's car that had tried to run her down and hopefully they had footage of him in the driver's seat. Attempted murder was something they could add to his charges. Did they also have the ID of those men who were killed at the lake house?

As soon as she slid into the front seat of his car, he said, "Did you trash your boyfriend's apartment while in the process of looking for something?"

Her blood ran cold. They thought she had done all that? "No. I told you yesterday that I found it that way. And, Ryan Castle is definitely not my boyfriend. He's tried to kill me twice now, possibly three times. You really have to stop calling him my boyfriend. It's jangling on my last nerve."

"When you told me about the state of his apartment yesterday, I made no comment until I checked with the people keeping it under surveillance. It wasn't like that earlier in the day and it was like that after they saw you leave."

"It's obvious the ones who trashed it were there at some time in between. Why would I ..."

"Why go there at all?" He started the car and pulled into the traffic flow.

"I just felt like I couldn't stand around, or sit around, and do nothing while he was getting further away. I was looking around his apartment among all the rubble. I was looking for a clue to his true identity and a clue to where he might have gone."

He glanced over at her. "You were breaching our agreement, and we now know who he is."

"We don't have an agreement in writing. That's what I've been asking you for."

"You're not supposed to go rogue and go off by yourself. Regarding the agreement, it's not going to happen if you do stupid things like this. I thought you were more sensible, level-headed, calculating even."

She could tell he was annoyed by how he was clutching the steering wheel, so she remained silent. When they were nearly at his office, she said, "I won't do it again."

"Good."

"What's happened?"

"I'll tell you once we're in my office."

She decided not to mention she was badly in need of coffee.

Soon, they were sitting in his office and he began, "I've got a few things to tell you. They managed to get a plate number from your photos of the car that tried to run you down. The car was registered to Ryan Castle even though we know that's not his real name."

"Good. I thought as much."

He looked at her skeptically as though he could see right through her. Did he know she already knew that?

She cleared her throat to cover the sound of her empty tummy rumbling. "What about those men killed at the lake house? Do we know who they are yet?"

"No. They're still working on it. We canvassed the surrounding businesses where you had your incident with Castle and we ended up getting CCTV footage of it. We now have a warrant out for his arrest."

She clapped her hands. "Finally!"

"Would you like to view it?"

"The warrant?"

"No." He frowned at her. "The CCTV."

"No thanks. I lived it. I don't need to see it again."

He gave a curt nod. "The other thing is, we have a development. A piece from the Welch jewelry collection has surfaced in London. Do you know what this means?"

"Wonderful! We're going to London? I could do with getting away from here." She was envisioning all the shopping she could do while she was there, and all the places they could visit.

"No."

"Oh, that's too bad. I love London. It's brimming with history and there are so many things to do and see. The shopping is the best. I'd love to go back there soon." When she saw his disapproving face, she straightened in her chair as she focused on the job at hand. "Ah, the wife isn't guilty? Is that what you're thinking?"

"It's looking more like she didn't take the jewelry. Or has she leaked a piece to make it look like a robbery, thus strengthening her cover story?"

"Could be. Which piece of jewelry are we talking about?"

He adjusted his computer keyboard and turned the monitor allowing her to see. "It was traced back to a dealer right here in New York. A pawnbroker no less."

An image appeared on the screen. "It's the Cleopatra bangle. The collection of diamond-set Egyptian-styled jewelry was commissioned in the fifties by a certain member of the British royal family for his wife's private collection. They were made by Serita, a famous jewelry brand. That bracelet and the other two pieces of the collection they bought at Sotheby's were the only pieces to make it into this country."

"Correct. You've done your homework."

"I have. It wasn't hard to find out."

"We traced the origin back to a local pawnbroker. His records show the bracelet came to him the day after the robbery. He then sold it to an English gentleman, who was here on holiday. From there, the bracelet traveled back to England where the new owner tried to put it into auction. It was a staff member at the auction house who knew from our alerts that the piece was stolen."

"Good. Very thorough."

He showed her another picture on his computer. "This is the ID that was given to the pawnbroker."

She stared at the name. "Boris Stackovich. I don't recognize that name." She looked up at him. "Do you?"

"No. It's a fake ID, but good enough to fool the dealer. It's in their best interests not to look too closely at these things."

"That's true and have you talked to the pawnbroker who did the deal?"

"That's where we're going right now. The police are trying to find a facial recognition match for the man posing as Boris Stackovich."

She inhaled sharply. Did she want to go along to meet with this dealer? What if she knew him? "What is the name of the person we're going to talk to?"

"Blackburn. David Blackburn. Do you know him?" With piercing eyes he studied her face.

She forced a smile, and then shook her head. "No." It was the truth and she was relieved.

"He claims he didn't know the bracelet was stolen, but it's a unique piece. He'll most likely be charged for receiving stolen goods. They're questioning him now. Then we'll have our turn."

"Good. I can't wait."

He looked at her curiously.

"I need to know what happened that night at the Welch household."

His lips turned upward. "You and me both."

Gretel excused herself for a quick trip to the bathroom.

When she was drying her hands, the door was flung open and Monica Blaze walked in and stood over her.

She looked at Monica. "Yes?"

Monica's gaze dropped to her quilted black Channel. "Nice bag." She ran her fingertips over it.

It was an awkward moment. "Thanks."

When their eyes locked again, Monica said, "Jack got hurt and that's your fault. You took him on a wild goose chase after your boyfriend. I have no idea what you told him, but I want you to know that I'm watching you."

"It wasn't like that."

"You might've fooled everyone else including Jack, but I know you haven't reformed. When you slip up, I'll be right there to take you down."

"Good luck with that." Gretel moved to the door, but Monica stepped in front of her.

"Leave Jack alone. He'd never be interested in a criminal like you."

"So you think he'd be interested in you?"

"Already is."

"Just move aside."

She lowered her face so it was one inch from Gretel's. "I'm watching every move you make."

It took every ounce of self-control for Gretel to keep her hands by her sides. If she were back in prison and another inmate had done this to her, that would be a whole different story with a very different outcome. "Jack's waiting for me. Maybe I should tell him we were having this conversation and that's what took me so long, hmmm?"

"If Jack gets hurt again, you'll pay." She then moved aside, and Gretel wasted no time in getting away from her.

As she walked back to Jack's office, she wondered if Jack and Monica did have something going on. If they did, it made perfect sense to keep it a secret since they were working together.

JACK AND GRETEL walked into the interview room to see a nervous-looking, balding, middle-aged man sitting down at a small table.

"Hello, Mr. Blackburn. I'm special agent Jack Fletcher from the FBI and this is my assistant."

Blackburn clasped his trembling hands on the table in front of him. "I'll tell you what I told them. I didn't know it was stolen. How could I possibly know? I'm not a mind reader."

Jack and Gretel sat down in front of him.

"The jewelry has been on the news and in the papers. You would've got an email from us. They were sent out to all dealers and pawnbrokers in the vicinity."

"I work all the time and don't look at those things. Am I going to be charged?"

Gretel had thought from what Jack said that the man had already been arrested.

Jack leaned forward. "I'm only interested in the man who brought the bracelet in. Did he say or do anything out of the ordinary?"

"No. He said he had something to sell. Said it belonged to his maiden aunt who'd just died. Said she died in an old people's home and this was fresh out of her bank safe deposit box. He said he wasn't married so he had no wife to give it to. All he wanted was enough money to get a set of golf clubs. I gave him enough to get a top of the line set."

"And you got it all on tape?" Gretel asked.

"Yes. It's all there on the footage. The woman who works for me downloaded it and gave it to the cops."

Jack handed over his card. "If you think of anything else, no matter how small, please call me."

He took the card and looked at it. "I will."

They left the police station after Jack was given a USB stick with the footage of the Cleopatra bracelet transaction. They also had footage of the seller getting into and out of a vehicle.

WHEN JACK and Gretel arrived back at his office, he put the stick into his computer with Gretel looking over his shoulder.

"He's got a hat on so it's hard to see his face. But

the interesting thing is what the police got from across the road at the bookstore. He gets back into a taxi with a woman." He froze the shot of the woman.

"Can you see a clear view of her face?"

"No, I can't. I'll have to send it off and see if they can enlarge it up and make it less grainy. Still, this is the best lead we've had so far. They're trying to lift fingerprints off the document he signed." He downloaded the file to his hard drive. "I'll give this to the IT guys in person. Back in a minute."

She quickly sat in his seat, opened his drawer, pulled out an empty data stick and started to download the file onto it. "Come on, come on, come on." She calmed her nerves the best she could. If he caught her, he'd never trust her—with good reason. Kent would be better than anyone on the FBI IT team, or just as good as, she knew.

The instant she saw the words, 'download completed,' she heard footsteps and saw the door handle move. Her heart felt like it was jumping right out of her chest.

Jack was back.

CHAPTER 21

GRETEL PULLED the USB stick from the computer, stood up and shoved it in her front pants pocket a millisecond before Jack walked back in. She looked up at him. "How long did they say it would take?"

"We should have something by tomorrow." He frowned at her being around his side of the computer.

She brushed dust off the top of the monitor hoping it would look like that was all she'd been doing. "Good."

Once she was sitting down on her usual chair, he sat back down at the computer. "Want a copy?"

"Sure." She had to smile, seeing the funny side. All that stress she'd just been through for nothing.

He pulled open his drawer and pulled out a USB stick from a packet. After he pushed it into his computer, he said, "Maybe you'll see something if you study it better. Take another look with me. I'll play it again while it's downloading."

She got up and walked back around to his side of the desk.

They both watched carefully, and Jack paused it on the woman in the taxi. Gretel said, "Sure is grainy, but the impression of that woman is that she's wealthy. Her clothes don't look cheap. That's for sure. The sunglasses are designer, too."

"How can you tell?"

"Instinct. All that dark hair isn't her own. She's making an attempt to disguise herself."

"Which leaves us where?"

"Someone, a female, has good taste in clothes and sunglasses, and she may or may not have black hair."

"We'll have to hope they can pull a fingerprint from the paperwork. Not likely, but we can hope. This is the best lead we've had so far," he repeated.

"Isn't it the only one you've had?"

He grinned. "That too."

He took the USB stick out of the computer and handed it to her.

"Thanks." She sat back down on the chair in front of his desk.

"There were no prints at the Welch household that shouldn't have been there. Staff, family. The staff didn't benefit from his death and they weren't even there that night. I've got surveillance tape of them at the hotel they'd been sent to by Mrs. Welch."

"Very convenient to get them out of the way. She stands to gain the most. If she did it, then she gets the insurance payout for the jewelry she probably still has, and his life insurance. And she doesn't have to go through a divorce and the scandal that would've gone along with it. She'd get a widow's sympathy and get to keep all her friends. Those who divorce lose half their friends, I'm told."

"Is that right?" He smirked.

"I used to listen in to my father counseling people. I got to hear all the gossip and all the tales of woe."

"How exactly did you hear that?"

"In the next room. It was a spare bedroom and my sister and I used to each put a drinking glass up against the wall and stand there with our ears pressed against them. It works. Sometimes we heard some things we didn't want to know."

"I can imagine. Well, that's all I have for you today. For homework, study that tape and see what you see."

"Thanks. I'll find my own way home if you're through with me today."

"I'll have someone drive you. We can't take any risks."

"I'll do my best." She stood. "Just as well I have protection."

"Protection from what?" Monica breezed into the room.

Gretel saw Monica was clutching two take-out

coffees. "Oh, that's so nice of you to bring me a coffee, Monica, but I was just leaving."

"Oh, you're leaving? Too bad. One's for Jack anyway, and one's mine."

The whine in Monica's voice was annoying. Gretel tried her best to control her urge to slap her. Not in front of Jack. Gretel looked back at Jack. "Bye."

"Wait. I'm organizing you a ride home."

She didn't want anyone but Jack to drive her. "I'm sure it'll be okay. I'll get a taxi straight home and lock my door."

"Call me the moment you're in your apartment so I don't worry."

"I will." Gretel saw Monica was upset over that last bit. Gretel gave her a beaming smile before she walked out.

Monica showing up like that had been rotten timing.

Jack was right about her having to be careful. Ryan wanted her dead, and those men at the lake house did, too.

Once she had gotten home and let Jack know she was there, she downloaded the footage of the man selling the Cleopatra bracelet and then emailed it to another of the emails she used. Any activity on her emails would trigger Kent's attention. In the body of the email, she wrote a 'note to self,' 'Find out who this man is and the woman in the car.'

Then being impatient, she disregarded Jack's warnings about staying home. If Ryan Castle really wanted her dead he would've shot her. Perhaps he was merely trying to warn her off—scare her off.

She grabbed her bag and headed to Kent's place, so she'd be right there when he found out who those people were. They were the key to the robbery and to who killed Glen Welch.

CHAPTER 22

WHEN SHE KNOCKED on his door, Kent opened it immediately. "Got him."

"The man on the tape?"

"Yes." Once she was inside, he closed and bolted the door behind her.

"Who is he?"

"Sullivan Manns."

The name didn't ring any bells. "Never heard that name. Where can I find him?"

"Last known address is right here." He told her the address. "We could walk there in ten minutes."

"What about the woman?"

"Can't get an ID on her yet. I'll keep working on it." Kent sat back down in front of his computer. "I didn't know you were coming here. Did you make sure you weren't followed?"

"I always do. I need to find out how that man got

the jewelry. Was he one of the robbers or did someone ask him to sell it? And who's that woman? How can I find out? I'd love to knock on his door and ask this Sullivan Manns fellow, but he wouldn't tell me."

"You've got that right. What you need are some thugs. If some beefy men show up at his door, he's more likely to spill all."

"I don't know. I'm not a fan of violence."

"No one is, but if you want the truth this might be the quickest way. Marty would know people."

"Okay, I'll call him. I need the truth, but only if no one's caught. Got a cell phone I can use?"

She'd already turned hers off on the drive there. He reached into his desk drawer, pulled one out and tossed it to her. She knew Marty's number by heart.

"Speak," Marty said.

Gretel was taken aback. "Marty, it's me."

"Ah, my desperate crooked friend. I haven't heard from you in a while."

She ignored his nonsense. "I'm with Kent." She gave him a quick rundown of the situation and what she wanted him to organize.

"Why can't you let the FBI handle it since you're now in cahoots?"

"I'm not in cahoots. I've got a nasty woman trying to get rid of me. She's got a mad crush on my boss. Not everyone's happy I'm there."

"I can't understand that." He chuckled.

"The point is I've been nearly killed thrice, so I want to know what's going on."

"'Thrice,' did you say? That's not good. You always have been a control freak. Need to have your hand in every pie, need to cross those Ts and dot those Is."

"So, do you know anyone threatening-looking who can knock on this guy's door and ask questions?"

"Does the sun come up every morning and go down every evening? You should know I do."

"Good. I don't want him hurt. I just want him to think he could be hurt so he'll tell them what they need to know."

"Have Kent email me the deets. I need to know what questions you want asked and nothing wishy-washy. We'll only get one go at this."

"Thanks, Marty. I owe you one."

"Hell no! I'm billing you for it and these guys won't come cheap. Later." He ended the call.

She turned to Kent. "He said—"

"I heard. Emailing him now." He turned back to his computer and tapped busily on the keys. "Done. Now, how about a movie and a pizza? The latest Batman movie's out. I've been saving up to watch it with someone."

She couldn't think of anything worse. She wasn't a fan of superheroes and she was trying to cut down on carbs. Still, she didn't have many friends and he had fewer. "Sounds great and I am a bit hungry."

A smile brightened his face. "I'll order the pizza."

"Did you send him the surveillance video to make sure they get the right person?"

"All done. Marty never replies. I'll check to see if he's opened it yet." He turned back to the computer. "Yep. All done."

She was relieved.

After her late night of batman movie watching and pizza eating, Kent accompanied her to her car. She drove home nervously, hoping she wouldn't see that black car again.

When she was back inside the safety of her apartment, she collapsed onto her bed. It took no time for her to fall asleep.

AT EIGHT THE NEXT MORNING, she opened her cell phone to see if there was any news from either Kent or Marty.

Before she could dial out, Kent was calling her.

"Hi."

"I have an email from Marty. His friends paid a late-night visit to Sullivan Manns. He spilled his guts. Marty's words not mine."

"Tell me."

"The man's a friend of Gizelle Butterworth and she gave it to him to sell." The phone dropped from her hands and she slid to the floor. Gizelle was Ryan's half-sister. They had the same father. She'd only just joined the dots. She grabbed hold of the phone. "Kent, do you realize that Ryan and Gizelle are half-siblings?"

"Gretel … don't tell me you've only just figured it out. You said he's a Butterworth and so's she. Earl Butterworth is their father."

She rubbed her head feeling like a fool. "It's so weird … and she's a friend of Hazel's. What are the odds of meeting her half-brother halfway around the world?"

"Truth is stranger than fiction. It's a small world, and all that."

"I'm an idiot for not seeing that sooner. I don't know why it didn't click."

"Hey, don't be so hard on yourself. You've had a lot going on with being in prison and everyone trying to kill you."

Gretel sighed. It wasn't everyone, but it felt like it. "That's true. If Gizelle is involved that means Ryan could've helped her."

"What are you going to do?"

"I'm going in to see Jack. I'll talk to you later." She got off the phone quickly and got ready for 'work.'

GRETEL WALKED into Jack Fletcher's office and put the man's name in front of him. "This is the guy who sold the Cleopatra bracelet, Sullivan Manns."

"Is that right?"

"Yes."

"I've just been notified of that. How did you find out?"

"I asked around." She gave a nervous cough hoping Jack wasn't going to insist she tell him more.

He didn't. He turned to his computer and tapped some keys and the man's rap sheet came up. "Minor drug charges. No theft."

"He's a friend of Gizelle's. She was the woman in the car."

He swung his chair around to face her. "Welch's stepdaughter? Butterworth's daughter. She goes by the last name of Welch, but she's not a Welch."

"That's right. Gizelle had Sullivan Manns do her dirty work. She had him take the bracelet in to sell it."

"That's new information." He turned back to his computer and as he tapped on the keys, he said, "I'm not even going to ask how you know that. Everything's got to be by the book. I'll have him picked up and brought in for questioning. Once he sees himself on the footage, he'll confess. Surely." He made a call while she paced around the room walking off her nervous energy. When he ended the call, he stared at her. "Now we wait. Once he mentions Gizelle, we'll go pick her up."

"We?"

"Yes."

"She knows me."

"This is the first time I'm hearing about that."

"I said one of Josephine's husbands was a contributor to my father's ministry and I told you I'd been to their house as a kid. Wait, that doesn't fit the timeframe. She must've been married to Welch when I was at the house. Maybe it was Glen Welch who donated to the ministry and not Butterworth." She rubbed her head. Most of her childhood was a blur and that was the way she preferred to keep it. There were so few happy memories.

"You said before, you knew each other as children, you and Gizelle?"

"That's right. We met when we were young. I have only seen her once briefly since then. I know my sister keeps in touch with her. She'd know who I am. That's why I was doing my best to make sure Gizelle and her mother didn't see me at the funeral, and I don't think they did."

"She doesn't have to see you."

She breathed easy. "Good."

"You can be in another room. The disadvantage of that is you won't be able to ask questions."

With a hand over her heart she sighed with relief. "I can live with that."

"It won't be happening today. By the time they find Sullivan Manns and bring him in, it'll be late this afternoon or even tonight. Then they'll pick up Gizelle tomorrow."

"I hope she's still in the country by then."

"I asked each member of the family not to leave town."

"Okay." She jumped to her feet. "I'll wait to hear from you tomorrow, then."

"Yes. I'll have someone drive you home. I've got paperwork I've got to finish."

"No. I'm okay."

He frowned at her. "I insist."

She shook her head. "Please don't fuss. I'm okay."

"Call me as soon as you get home then."

"Okay." She turned and walked out of his office. When she continued past Monica's office, she felt the agent staring at her.

IT WAS eight o'clock in the morning when Jack called. "Gizelle is being interviewed at two today."

"Okay, I'll be there. No need to send someone for me. I was all right last night and I'll be all right today. I don't need a babysitter."

"Be in my office at one." She heard the click of him ending the call. He seemed upset or maybe it was just that he was busy.

When she arrived at his office, he wasn't there. Right on one, she got a text to say he was running late.

How late? she wondered as she pushed the phone back into her pocket.

She got out of the chair and closed his office door.

He had to be at least ten minutes away to have thought to notify her. Wanting to get to know him better, she sat behind his desk and opened his two drawers.

The left side drawer had nothing but stationery, but when she opened the right side, there was a thick file. She pulled it out and opened it. Her heart nearly stopped when she saw one newspaper clipping after another. These were her robberies. Of course she wasn't mentioned by name. Until now she'd been convinced no one knew the length and breadth of everything she'd done. Wrong. Here it was, all documented and all in one place. He'd been aware of her. She looked through the dates of the articles. They went back four years.

She was frozen, staring down at them wondering why he hadn't mentioned he knew this much about her. He'd referred to her crimes but not in any detail. She'd been right not to let her guard down with him.

The other thing that ran through her mind was, why did he leave it in his drawer like that? Was he hoping she'd come across it? Did anyone else know about his file?

Either way, it didn't sit well with her. She placed all the clippings back in the folder where they'd been and returned it to the drawer. When she was back on 'her' side of the desk, she opened a file on the Glen Welch case. She flipped through the pages until she found the identity of the man they found drunk at the Welch house the night she was there. There was a whole sheet on him along with his photo and, going by the address, he was a neighbor of Glen Welch. He looked to be in his seventies. This was definitely not the man who'd grabbed her foot that night.

She closed the file and then thought she should open the door. If Jack arrived to see the door closed he'd think it strange.

When she opened it, Jack was right there in front of her with his hand on the handle.

Think fast. "Here you are. I've been waiting for you. I had the door shut because I felt odd sitting there alone with you not being here. Some of these people around here intimidate me."

He smiled as she stepped back into his office. "I told you not to worry about Monica."

"How did you know I was talking about her?"

"It wasn't hard. Sorry to keep you waiting. I needed to follow up on a few leads." He sat behind his desk and since he didn't say where those leads were or what they were, she had to wonder if it was about her.

"That's okay. Is Gizelle coming here or will she be at the police station?"

"At the station. The way the traffic is, we'd be better off walking."

"Oh, right now?"

He tapped a few keys on his computer. "I'll just check my emails and then we can go."

"I could've met you there."

"Better that we arrive together."

"Ah, yes of course." She sat quietly and waited for him to finish what he was doing.

They walked together as much as they could while weaving in and out of the busy lunchtime pedestrians. It was hard to keep up with Jack's long strides and she was grateful she'd worn semi-comfortable shoes rather than the stilettos she had nearly chosen.

When they arrived at the station, they met Officer Harvey and Seargent Wilkes who were interviewing Gizelle. Then they were ushered to a room where they could watch people being interviewed.

Gretel sat on a chair while Jack sat on the desk next to her. "Let's hope she doesn't bring a lawyer with her."

"I'd be surprised if she didn't," Gretel said.

Right on time, they watched through the two-way mirror as Gizelle and a man in a suit were shown into the interview room.

Jack said, "That's Glen Welch's brother again."

"It makes sense she'd bring him since her mother is using him as her lawyer, too. Keeping it in the family I suppose."

Seargent Wilkes pushed a photo of Sullivan Manns toward her. "Do you know this man?"

"I do. I gave him my mother's bracelet to sell. It's not a crime. My mother would've given it to me if I'd asked her."

Officer Harvey picked up a sheet of paper. "Maybe so except it was listed among the stolen goods in the paperwork that your mother gave us and her insurance company. That *is* a problem. Why did you sell it?"

Reginald Welch, acting as her lawyer, said, "You don't have to answer that."

"It's okay. I've got nothing to hide. The truth was I needed the money. Things have been tough."

"How did you come by it?"

She moved uncomfortably in the seat. "I ... borrowed it, some time ago, and Mom forgot I had it."

"Were you aware your friend offered a false ID in order to sell the bracelet?"

"How would I know he'd do that? I'm not a good negotiator, so that's why I sent him in."

Gretel whispered to Jack, "His story was he only wanted enough money to buy a set of golf clubs. Hardly a good negotiating tactic. She's lying."

"Yes, and he had that story about the maiden aunt in a nursing home."

"Are you going to charge me with something?" The defiance in Gizelle's voice was clearly evident. She knew they couldn't touch her with the story she'd concocted.

"I'll be back in a minute."

The officer joined Jack and Gretel in the room. "Would you like to ask a few questions, Agent Fletcher?"

"Yes, I would." Jack left the room and the officer stayed in the room with Gretel.

The officer and Gretel looked on. Every question

Jack asked was blocked by the lawyer. Gizelle had no comment to make about anything. Ten minutes later, Jack was back in the room with Gretel and Officer Harvey.

"I'm sure I could've got her to talk if it wasn't for her lawyer. How long do you think you can keep her here today?" Jack asked Harvey.

"Couple of hours, tops. Unless her lawyer gets impatient."

"Keep her for as long as you can. I just want to talk to her mother before Gizelle gets a chance to contact her. It's an hour's drive from here."

"You'd better get started."

Gretel and Jack walked out the door.

"What are you thinking?" Gretel asked on the way to the car.

"I think I was about to ask you what you thought."

"Sounds to me like her mother's guilty. It was an inside job. Gizelle is a bad liar."

"Do you think that piece was leaked to make the robbery look genuine?"

"Possibly. But it does seem a bit odd that she'd be so involved in the sale of it. Sitting in the car like she was. Unless she didn't trust him. That could be it. I mean the piece is worth a few hundred thousand so she might've been making sure he did exactly what he was told. That's why she was watching him, I guess, to make sure he got the job done."

They got into his car. "I'll be interested to see what

Josephine has to say about this bracelet and I hope we get there before Gizelle forewarns her."

"I'm thinking if Gizelle is involved in her stepfather's death, then might Sullivan Manns, who sold the bracelet, be an associate of the man who pulled the trigger?"

"It's possible."

"I think so. How many criminals would they know?"

Jack glanced at her. "Her husband was a lawyer."

Gretel had to smile. He had a good point.

When they arrived at the Welch mansion, the maid who answered the door showed them to a living room where they waited for Josephine. As Gretel sat there, she couldn't stop thinking about the way she'd left the safe, with the top of that secret section lying against the wall. The family had covered up that fact, unless they hadn't noticed it. Now she was going to come face-to-face with Josephine Welch after she'd been sneaking about in her home.

Josephine walked into the room with a flourish and Gretel and Jack stood. Gretel wasn't sure if the etiquette was that she should've stood too, but Josephine's presence seemed to demand it. Her golden-brown hair was perfectly piled on top of her head and her makeup was flawless. "Ah, Agent Fletcher." She reached out her hand and Jack shook it.

"Yes, and this is .."

She looked at Gretel with a spark of recognition. "Hazel?"

Gretel smiled. "Not quite. That's my sister."

"I knew you were one of the Koch girls. Wait, you're Gretel?"

Gretel was prepared for a bad reaction. That was why she hadn't wanted to see Mrs. Welch. It would also get back to her parents, and Gretel didn't want her parents to know anything about her.

"Ms. Koch is helping us with our inquiries," Jack said, with a smile.

"Oh, well, do take a seat."

"Would you prefer I not be here?" Gretel wondered if Jack might be better off questioning Josephine without her there.

"No that's perfectly fine."

Jack began, "I have some questions to ask you."

"Go ahead."

"Was your Cleopatra bracelet definitely stolen?"

"Yes. It was. I gave you the list. It's not here. Do you want to search the place?" She drew her eyebrows together, marring her perfectly smooth face.

"Your daughter tells us something different."

"Gizelle?"

He nodded.

"What about her?"

"We happen to know she was involved with the sale of the Cleopatra bracelet the day after the robbery."

"*My* Cleopatra bracelet?"

"That's right."

"But that was stolen in the robbery. It was in the safe."

"Your daughter tells a different story," Jack said.

Josephine's eyes grew wide as they fixed on Jack. "Gizelle? What did she say?"

"Do you know for sure it was in the safe?"

Josephine's fingers twirled the long rope of pearls around her neck. Then she looped a twist over one finger, slowly moving it side to side. The pearls made a soft clicking sound as they slid across one another, as if echoing the thoughts clicking through her mind. "I suppose I couldn't be one hundred percent sure."

"She says you let her borrow it some time ago, and she hadn't returned it."

"If she says I did, I must've. Is that really what she said, or do I need my lawyer again?"

Jack shook his head. "I'm not trying to trap you here. I'm merely asking some simple questions."

Trying to calm the situation, Gretel asked, "Mrs. Welch, would you mind if we take another look at the room where the safe is located?"

"Right now?"

"Yes, if you don't mind."

"I don't mind at all."

Together they walked up the stairs to the study.

Gretel walked over to the safe and stood in front of it. Her peripheral vision showed that the items she'd left between the safe and the wall were gone. She spun around to face Jack and Mrs. Welch. "This is a heavy safe. I'm guessing this floor is concrete?"

"Of course it is. Otherwise a safe like that wouldn't be supported. It had to be craned in through the window."

Gretel took another look around the room.

"Is that all? I don't like being in this room since this is where he was found."

"I'm sorry, Mrs. Welch. I wasn't thinking. We don't need to see anything more here."

As they walked back down the stairs, Jack said, "Is there anything you want to tell us about your husband's death, Mrs. Welch?"

"I told you everything I know." When they reached the bottom of the stairs she stopped and stared at Jack. "What are you implying, Agent Fletcher?"

"I'm implying nothing, Ma'am, I'm merely asking the question. These questions have to be asked."

"And those questions have already been asked *and* I have already answered them. I'm an upstanding person, I'm not some riffraff like you're used to dealing with." She glared at Gretel and then looked back at him. "You come into my home throwing wild accusations about me ..." her voice trailed off. "When did you talk to Gizelle?"

"Mrs. Welch, what do you think the insurance company will think now that they know your daughter had a piece of jewelry that was on the list as stolen?"

Gretel asked. "They'll take a closer look at the whole claim."

Josephine fiddled with the back of her hair. "I'm an honest person. From everything I know, that piece was in the safe ... unless it wasn't. Unless Gizelle had it, but I don't know why she would be selling it if she did have it. Surely, she would've said something. I'll talk to her and sort everything out and if she's got the bracelet I'll call the insurance company and tell them that particular piece wasn't taken."

Jack asked, "Do you know anyone by the name of Sullivan Manns?"

"No it doesn't sound familiar. Is he a TV actor?"

"No. He's the man your daughter had go into the pawnshop to offload your bracelet while she waited outside in a taxi."

Josephine glowered at Jack for a moment before she spoke again. "Are you telling me the truth or are you trying to trick me?"

"Believe me, it's the truth."

"It's all on tape," Gretel added. "We've seen the surveillance footage."

"Mrs. Welch, what do you think about when I say the word divorce?"

Gretel froze, sensing a definite chill in the room as Josephine's eyes flashed with ice-cold rage. "What are you implying?" She leaned against the end of the bannister as they continued to stand in the foyer at the bottom of the stairs.

"We have it on good authority that you were considering divorcing Glen Welch."

"I felt like divorcing him every other day. Marriage is not easy. Are you married, Agent Fletcher?"

He rubbed his forehead. "No, I'm not."

"And you're not are you, Gretel dear? Otherwise you wouldn't need to steal your diamonds. You'd simply have a rich husband and have him buy you what you want."

Gretel opened her mouth in shock. She hadn't stolen due to lack of a husband or due to lack of finances.

"If you … if either of you were married, you'd know marriages don't always run smoothly. My husband was a dreadful snorer. Which is why you'll notice we had separate bedrooms."

"I noticed that," Jack said. "But that's becoming more common these days."

"I didn't know that. I don't know who the trouble-maker is who told you I wanted to divorce Glen. Probably one of my so-called friends, was it?"

"I'm sorry, I can't say."

"Or were you just fishing for information, hmm? Trying to trap me into saying something?" Josephine brought her hands together and tapped her index fingers against each other.

Gretel was amazed at the woman. She had an answer for everything.

"I'm not 'fishing for information,' but the person

who told us was of the opinion that you were seriously considering it, and it wasn't just that you had gone through a rough day within the marriage."

"It's rubbish."

"You do stand to benefit quite a bit from your husband's life insurance and that came at the right time since his business was suffering and close to folding."

"I can't help the timing of it."

Jack asked, "Have you thought of anybody who could have been mad at you or your husband? Anyone who showed an interest in your jewelry?"

"First of all, everyone was interested in our jewelry. We beat a lot of people in the auction to get those pieces and paid top dollar. We were always having photographers here to photograph them for various magazines. You'd know all about them wouldn't you, Gretel?"

"Yes, you had a wonderful collection. One that many people envied."

"The sad thing is my mother-in-law's collection went too. She was a woman with a love of Art Deco jewelry. So many pieces we had could never be replaced by mere money. You can't put a price on sentiment."

"What about people who were upset with either you or your husband?"

As Gretel stood there listening, she wondered what it had been like for young Ryan, cast aside and forgotten about in some far-off boarding school. Had rejection turned him into a psychopath, or was he born one?

"Everyone was mad at my husband. He was a lawyer." She smiled, seeming almost proud of her own statement. "He had people upset with him every single day."

"What about closer to home? Friends?" Jack asked.

"I can't think of anything, except my husband's manservant was upset a while back. My husband had solid gold, diamond-encrusted cufflinks that went missing and he accused the manservant of taking them. When he found them days later, he remembered that he'd gotten home quite late and placed them in his sock drawer instead of putting them away properly. By the next morning he'd forgotten about them. It was all very silly, but Glen's comments offended him, and he nearly left over it. I had to offer the man more money to stay and of course my husband fell over himself apologizing for the incident. He felt so bad. But they wouldn't be involved, neither of them, either him or his wife who's our maid. They're both loyal staff members."

"We've talked to them already, but it wouldn't hurt to have another word with them. They could've remembered something they didn't mention before."

"Good."

"But they weren't so loyal, were they, if your husband thought what he did about them?"

Gretel was surprised at the way Jack poked a sharp

question in here and there. She never would've been brave enough to say such a thing to Josephine.

"It wasn't so much that, but there was no one else around who could've taken those cufflinks."

"What about cleaning staff?" asked Gretel.

"We have the cleaners in twice a week. They were due to come the very next day, so that's why it couldn't have been one of them."

"Any other information before we talk to your daughter once more?" Jack asked.

"She's not involved in any of this. My husband and she were very close if that's your next question."

"Pardon me if I have to disagree with that. There are witnesses who tell us they had words at a recent fundraising event."

Again, with Jack's tough comments.

Josephine didn't take offense at this, but neither had she directed them to sit down again. "Every family has little spats every now and again. Mine is no different. It didn't mean that she didn't have a deep love for her stepfather. After her own father died when she was little, Glen is the only father she's ever known."

"And what was the cause of your first husband's death, just out of interest? I know he was a lovely man and donated to my father's ministry." Gretel asked, smiling and looking as sweet as possible. Although, she wasn't quite sure which of Josephine's husbands did the donating. It was even possible it had been both.

"Yes, he did, Gretel. He got along with your father

very well. Earl went away on a fishing trip one weekend with some friends. Two of them didn't come back. Three were found alive but unfortunately the other two didn't make it and one was Earl." She looked down and Gretel felt bad for asking.

"I'm sorry to hear that," Jack said.

"Yes, I'm sorry too," Gretel added.

"But life goes on and we make the best of the life God gives us. Have I answered all your questions now, Agent Fletcher?"

"Yes you have and I'm sorry if any of our questions upset you. We are doing our best to get the jewels back for you and find out who killed your husband. I hope you understand that we were thrown a curveball when we tracked down the bracelet to your daughter."

"Thank you. I do appreciate that. Do you have the time for a cup of tea?"

"Not today, thank you, but would you mind if we come back tomorrow and talk with your staff?"

"That's fine. It's just the two of them. Julia Tuens and her husband, Phillipe. They live in the house to the left. Of course you'll know all that since you've already spoken to them."

"Yes they have been questioned extensively. Phillipe is the one your husband thought took his cufflinks?"

Josephine's dark lashes flickered. "That's right, but it's maybe best not to mention that. He takes things to heart. It took him a long time to get over Glen thinking he'd done it."

"Noted." Jack smiled.

Gretel stared at the woman. It seemed more and more likely that there was no robbery. It had been staged so no one would look too closely at Glen's death.

"I'll show you out. I've given both Julia and Phillipe the rest of the day off, but they'll be back on duty tomorrow. The maid who let you in today is someone new I'm trying out. This is her first day."

They said their goodbyes, left the house, and got into the car.

"Do you believe her about anything she said?" Gretel asked Jack.

"Do you?" He started the car.

"No."

"She's guilty of something, but exactly which part?"

Gretel looked back at the house as they drove away.

"What part of it didn't you believe, Gretel?"

"If you ask me, the only thing she's telling the truth about is that her first husband died."

Jack laughed. "He did, but she didn't even tell the entire truth about that."

As they drove out the gates, Gretel stared at him. "What is the rest of the truth?"

"Husband number two—Glen Welch, our victim— was the one who owned the boat. He was hosting the weekend of fishing when the two men were killed."

CHAPTER 23

GRETEL STARED AT JACK, processing the information he'd just delivered. Josephine Welch's second husband was on the boat when her first husband died. What a coincidence. "I had no idea. You would've thought she'd have said something about that."

"It wasn't hard to find out, so it's odd that Josephine didn't come right out and tell us. It was all over the papers at the time."

"I'd love to know more about it."

"I can pull them up on the computer for you when I get back to the office." He made a call to the officer who'd been holding Gizelle only to be told that she and her step-uncle lawyer had just left.

As soon as he ended the call, Gretel said, "Glen owned the boat, Earl died and then Glen married Earl's widow. I could let my imagination run wild there."

"Yes, but remember, we're dealing in facts and facts

are not facts unless we have the evidence to prove they are. I'll pull the file on the accident and see what it says."

"Good. And notice how she threw her servants under the bus? There was no need to mention the cuff-links incident. Seems she was diverting unwanted attention to her poor old servants."

"Maybe she was nervous, and her mouth ran away with her."

"It's possible I suppose. Jack, do you think there would be a day soon when you don't need me? I've got some things to take care of."

"Like what?"

She wasn't expecting him to be so intrusive. "Errands."

"Personal errands?"

"That's right." She held out her fingernails. "I haven't had these redone since I've been out of prison, and it was a while before that when they were done last."

"They look fine to me."

"They're dreadful."

He shook his head. "There will be plenty of time for that later. Don't forget someone wants you out of the way. I think errands can wait. I'll order us Chinese. We can eat and then dig into the files."

"Don't I need to be classified or something to look at the documents, look in the files?"

"I say you can, that's good enough." She stared at

him and he glanced over at her. "What do you want? Holy water sprinkled on you?"

"No, please, anything but." She giggled. "I might disappear."

"They're not that confidential. They're murder files and they're not leaving my office. You're merely reading them under my watch."

"Okay. That's good enough for me. What if Josephine was having an affair with the second husband before the first husband died?"

"That would be motivation for Glen to do away with the first husband. It would go from being an accident into a homicide, but our suspect is dead, so ..."

"What about the other man who was killed? Did Glen also have a reason for getting rid of him, a two-for-one deal? Or maybe that man saw something he wasn't supposed to see. He was a liability who became a casualty."

"The possibilities are endless." He shot her a smile. "Why don't we wait until we read the file?"

"Okay." She was pleased to have more time alone with Jack so she could get to know him better. Then she might find out what was behind him collecting those news articles of her robberies.

"Tell me, why did you want to see the study again?"

"Just to get a feel for what went on there. Reacquaint myself with the layout and such."

"And?"

She shrugged her shoulders. "Nothing new occurred

to me if that's what you mean." All kinds of possibilities had flown through her mind, but nothing she intended to tell him. The most likely was that Josephine found those sections between the safe and the wall, thought that the police had left it like that, and had her servants put them back before she closed it up.

With lightning speed, Gretel's gaze whizzed over the news reports about Earl Butterworth's unfortunate death.

Men missing. Five men went out in the boat for a day of fishing, even though there'd been rough seas all week. Earl Butterworth and Edward Cavallaro both went missing. Seems the fell off the side of the boat in the high seas.

Both bodies washed up within five miles of each other on the same day.

"Edward Cavallaro. That's the name of the other man who was killed besides Josephine's first husband." Gretel took out her phone and snapped a picture of the name. "Like I said, maybe Edward Cavallaro saw something he shouldn't have, like Earl Butterworth being knocked over the head and pushed off the boat."

"We might never find out."

"What do the other men who were in the boat at the time say?"

"I talked to the detective who was on the case at the time. The other men on the boat were all drunk and don't remember a thing. They woke up and Earl and Edward were both gone."

"That's no help. Sounds like more of a drinking trip than a fishing trip. What did the detective think about it all?"

"No proof of any wrongdoing. Glen Welch said he wasn't drinking but he wasn't feeling well so he was asleep too. When he woke, he noticed the two men were missing and it was he who raised the alarm."

"How do we find out how friendly Glen was with Josephine before her husband died?"

"That might be difficult. She's going to deny it and I don't think we'll find the proof. Even if they were having an affair at the time, that doesn't mean Glen pushed poor old husband number one off the boat."

She sighed. "What If Glen suddenly confessed to killing husband one and Josephine was outraged and plotted to kill Glen?"

He smiled. "Not likely to have kept silent all these years. We have to keep asking, keep poking around until we find something. This aside, our main focus has to be on the case at hand, not what we think might've happened in the past."

"Where does finding Ryan Castle fall on the attention scale?"

"Right up there at the top. I'm focused on that too and even more so with him connected to this case, but we can't do anything until he surfaces again. We're waiting and watching. Trust me, it's under control. You're out of prison, you just have to make sure you stay out." He pointed at her. "Don't do anything silly like going off on your own."

"I wouldn't."

"You already have. You went to Ryan's apartment."

"Oh that. Okay, I won't do anything like that again. When can I get an official pardon, one in writing?"

"It's underway."

"I guess I'll have to trust you on that one."

"Yes." He reached over and gave her another handful of papers. "Read."

She took them from him and looked at the first page. "How about you check to see if Josephine's got safe deposit boxes somewhere? Maybe she's visited them recently."

"It's been checked. We can't find she's got any."

"She wouldn't risk hiding jewelry in the house. I wonder if she has a really good friend she can trust?"

"It'd have to be a particularly good friend. One who wouldn't ask what she was doing and could be entrusted with a fortune."

"And I imagine friends like that would be hard to come by."

"I'd say so."

Gretel put her head down and kept reading.

. . .

WHEN IT STARTED to get dark, Jack suggested he take her home. It was Friday night and Gretel wondered if he had somewhere to be. A date perhaps? Hopefully not with Monica.

On the drive to her house, he suggested that she have a break tomorrow since it was Saturday.

"Are you having a day off too?" she inquired.

"I'm going to do my best. A break might clear my head. Clear both our heads. It never usually works out, though. I'm usually called in over something or other."

"A break sounds good. I've got so many things to catch up on."

As soon as she got home, she called her sister. She needed to speak to someone normal and her sister was the most normal person she knew.

Hazel couldn't talk, but promised she'd stop by the next morning and bring breakfast.

CHAPTER 24

GRETEL STARED at her sister who was sitting on the opposite couch in Gretel's living room. "I wonder why Ryan's been so hard to find. He's gone completely off the radar. Even the FBI can't find him."

"Perhaps he died and he's lying out there somewhere."

"I've already considered that. If he'd died then the body would show up. There's been no news."

"But strange, you said he had been at the lake house."

Gretel nodded as she thought back to the dreadful time at the lake house. "Someone had been there. It might not have been him. I know he's alive because he tried to run me down."

"That's really awful. I couldn't believe that when you told me."

"I have bad judgment with men, it seems." Gretel

looked down into her black coffee. She didn't really feel like drinking it.

"How well did you even know him before you got involved with him?"

She sighed. "Not well enough obviously. We met in Rome when he was in the middle of a sting. I watched, knowing what he was doing. He was a thief, but not my kind. I could never look anybody in the eye like he could and lie to them."

Hazel scoffed. "You were pretty good at lying when we were younger."

"Only if it was a choice between telling a lie and getting the strap. And, I had a guilty conscience every time I lied. Ryan has no conscience."

Hazel brought her legs up onto the couch and sat cross legged. "Are you going to go straight now?"

"Yes. I really don't have any other choice. Now they know who I am, they're watching my every move."

"What made you get into doing this? You've never given me a proper answer."

"It's just that this system is unfair and it's run by men. People have turned into puppets. The laws are weighted so no one thinks for themselves and no one can get ahead financially with all the silly rules. I simply didn't want to be one of the pack being told what to think, being told what to do. I for one don't want to be what they want us to be."

"Oh, Gretel. You're just doing what you want, aren't you? Then making some stupid excuse to make it look like someone else is to blame. Dad always said you never took responsibility."

"You asked me, and I told you. There are people who control everything, the world."

"So your solution is to steal?"

Gretel smiled at her younger sister by one year. "It makes sense to me. That way I don't fit into the mold."

"Mom told me not to go anywhere near you or I'll get influenced by you."

"Nice to know she thinks so highly of me."

"Influenced, not in a good way," Hazel told her.

"I know exactly what she meant. She never did like me. I used to think I was overlooked, but now I know she was overlooking me because she didn't like what she saw."

"That's not so, Gretel. I don't know why you think so badly of them. They're not that awful."

Gretel laughed. Her sister preferred to see things like that because she was still living with them. "Let's agree to disagree. Better yet, let's not talk about them at all."

"That's probably best."

"You know that I'm working on the Welch case?"

"Yes, you told me already."

"You're still good friends with Gizelle, right?"

"I haven't seen her in a long time. We were never that close, but we do share a lot of the same friends. She's in my group of friends. I didn't go to Glen's funeral. I don't like funerals."

"Your social life sounds very complicated. Anyway, no one likes funerals."

Hazel's cell phone beeped, and she pulled it out of her bag. "Ah, got to go."

"Really?"

"Yes. I've got a date tonight with someone new." Hazel smiled as she looked at her phone, and then her fingers got busy texting someone back.

Gretel's sister had only been gone two minutes when Gretel's phone sounded. It was from a 'no caller ID.' "Hello."

"Now that your sister's gone, make sure you're not being followed and meet me at our café in ten minutes."

The call ended. Her heart raced at a million miles a minute.

She knew the voice.

It was Ryan Castle.

CHAPTER 25

GRETEL THREW the phone onto the couch. He was watching her. How did he know Hazel was her sister? They'd never met. And, he knew she was alone in her apartment.

Her hand went to her stomach to still the nausea swirling and she moved to the window and looked out. As her eyes traveled over the trees in the park and the other buildings in the street, she knew there were so many places he could be hiding. The nausea overcame her and she ran to the bathroom, heaving.

She leaned over the toilet and was sick. When she was done, she rinsed her mouth out and looked at herself in the mirror.

Ech. That was what she felt when she saw her white face with dark mascara smudges under her eyes. With a moistened swab, she removed the smudges, and then applied blush and lippy to make her feel more human.

What he'd referred to as 'their café' was a brisk five-minute walk away. She grabbed her bag, threw in her phone and set off. A million questions raced through her mind.

Was he finding it hard to move such large stones and he needed her connections?

Was he going to offer to split the haul with her, and apologize for branching out and going solo?

Apologize for abandoning her to drown in the car like a rat going down with a sinking ship?

Would he have some excuse for nearly running her over with his car?

Each step on the pavement pounded inside her head as her heart continued to race. The disconcerting thing was, part of her wanted him to suffer and be out of her life completely, another part of her wanted to be held in his arms. It was sick to miss him and hate him at the same time. She couldn't go back in time to the way things were.

Just as the café came into sight, she decided that she had to be crazy right now. Why was she meeting him at all?

She stood on the other side of the road and looked through the floor-to-ceiling glass that made up the front of the café. He wasn't at their usual table by the window. Maybe he wanted to sit in the back to talk. She dashed across the road to the café as soon as there was a break in the traffic. When she pushed through the open doors of the coffee shop, a quick look around the room told her that he was nowhere.

Her first reaction was that it had been a cruel trick. Was he merely playing with her, pulling her strings as though she were a puppet just because he could? She glanced down at the time on her cell phone. Still five minutes to go.

She sat down at the first table she came to and waited, drumming her fingertips on the table while looking around. She hated that there was a tiny part of her looking forward to seeing him, swirling amongst the parts filled with fear. Maybe she needed therapy.

"Hi, Gretel."

Gretel looked up to see the young waitress that often served her.

"Hello, Dee."

"Your friend said to give you this."

Gretel took the note from her. "My friend?"

"Yes, the man you often come here with."

"Thank you." She didn't want to open the note in front of Dee.

"Will it be the usual today?"

"No, thanks, I'm not staying." She opened the note when Dee walked away. It was an address somewhere on the other side of town. Under it, he'd told her to go there, and to leave immediately.

A half-hour taxi drive later, Gretel stood looking up at a warehouse. Since Ryan was nowhere to be seen, she walked around trying to find a way in figuring he might be waiting for her inside. There was no way she was walking into that place to be alone with him. What she planned was to coax him outside to talk.

On the side of the building was a sad-looking, rusty red roller door with half the paint peeling off. She leaned down and pulled on the handle. To her surprise it opened.

Someone came from behind her and before she could turn around, large hands grabbed her, pushed her inside, and pulled the door down.

Just like that, her plan was ruined.

In the dark gloominess of the deserted space, she stood looking up into the deep green hazel eyes of Ryan Castle. Locked in his gaze, so many questions raced through her mind.

He pulled her in against his hard chest. "I've missed you, babe."

She pushed him as hard as she could. "Get away from me. What's this all about?"

"You're free, I'm free and we have the diamonds."

She was pleased he still had the diamonds. There was a chance he'd be caught. "Are you crazy or do you just have the shortest memory of any person on earth?"

He said nothing, and his eyes opened wider.

"I'm talking about you trying to run me down in the street. Why would you do that?"

He tried to touch her hair and she put up her hand to stop him. "I found out you were working with the FBI and I thought you'd turned on me."

"How could I? I clearly know nothing about you. And you left me to drown in that car as well. You knew I couldn't open the door of the car until it was completely submerged. Do you know how scary that was? I still have nightmares about it. I told you I wasn't a good swimmer."

"I thought that was an exaggeration. You know how you're always telling stories. Every time you tell a story it gets better."

"What about the lake house? Did you have anything to do with that shooting? Wait! Why am I asking you, the biggest liar on earth?"

"I heard about the shooting at the lake house." He shook his head. "There are people after me, and you too, it seems. You shouldn't have gone there."

She stared at him trying to work out if he was trying to scare her. When she'd been shot at, she had hoped it was only because she was there with Jack Fletcher. "What people are after you?"

"How would I know?"

Gretel wanted to scream. "You just said people are after both of us. Who were those people with guns? They pulled up in two white SUVs."

"I've got no idea."

He was still a liar, still keeping things from her.

"You were shot at and I had my place ransacked and it wasn't the police, that's all I know."

He tried to run over her, but right now she had to

know about Glen Welch. "Did you have anything to do with the robbery at the Welches' place?"

He frowned. "No! Of course not."

"Don't look so surprised. There was no love lost with you and your stepfather. Seems no one wanted you around."

"You have done your homework."

"Where are the diamonds?"

"In a safe place."

"What do you plan to do with them?"

"'What do *we* plan to do with them,' you should be asking. They're ours."

Now that she was face-to-face with him, she wished she had called Jack Fletcher. It was dumb of her to think she could handle Ryan Castle by herself. Then she realized she still had her cell phone in her bag that was slung over her shoulder, and she hoped Jack was tracking her through it. She fanned her face. "I'm getting hot. I feel like I'm going to faint. Can you open a window?"

"I'll try." While he walked to the window, she dove into her bag, fumbled for her phone and pressed Jack's number that she had on speed dial. Then she followed him to the window. He tried to open it, but it wouldn't budge.

"No go, sorry."

"Ryan, why don't you cut the nonsense and tell me where the diamonds are?"

"How do I know I can trust you now that you're best buddies with the feds?"

"I'm not. That's the only way I could get out of going back to prison. What was I going to do, turn down my only chance?"

Ryan threw his head back and laughed and she wanted to hurt him for hurting her.

"Where have you been staying?" she asked.

"I can't tell you that until I know I can trust you."

"What do you want from me?"

"In exchange for half the diamonds I want the name of a fence who'll be able to move big stones and other things. I know you've got contacts you've never shared with me."

"Other things? Do you mean like the Welch collection?"

He stepped closer and loomed over her and she sensed the threat when his body tensed. "I need the name of your fence—the best one."

"And then what? You'll give me half of something that's rightfully mine anyway?"

"Right now what have you got, Gretel? A big zero, a big zilch, a big nothing. If you help me, I'll drop half on you. If you don't, I'll find my own fence eventually and you'll get nothing."

"Since you're a liar and a thief what guarantee do I have that you won't stiff me like you did last time? I've heard that the definition of stupidity is doing the same thing over and over and expecting a different result."

His lips turned upward into a smile. "You have my word, babe."

She walked toward the door hoping that Jack was on his way. "But you see, the word of a liar is quite unreliable."

"It's not personal, this is business."

"It was personal though. We were supposed to love each other."

"I do love you, Crystal, and I want us to be together."

Her mouth dropped open in shock. "It's Gretel." No wonder he called her babe all the time. It was easier than making the effort to remember her name. "Who's Crystal?"

"No one. I'm sorry. She was my past and I want you to be my future. Come away with me. Let's go together." He took a step toward her and she pushed him hard with both hands.

"Get away from me."

"Don't be like that."

"I wish I'd never met you."

"Hey, I didn't come after you in Rome. You chased after me."

She walked towards the door and when she was halfway there, she turned around. "I've never chased anyone. You're probably thinking about Crystal."

"You approached me in that casino in Rome, not the other way around."

"What does that have to do with anything?" As

much as she wanted to leave, she had to delay things, so Jack had time to get there. She sure hoped that he would be able to locate her. Or had she accidentally turned off her phone by bumping it?

He walked forward and put his hands on her shoulders. "I'm sorry, all right? I'm sorry for everything. Let's put the past in the past and let's get on with things. You must admit in our game it's difficult to trust people, but now I'm sure I can trust you."

"You admit you left me in the car to die and tried to run me down?"

"I said that. Yes, and I am sorry. It wasn't planned. Both were heat of the moment things."

"If I'd tried to kill you—"

"Enough already!" he yelled showing the temper she knew had been bubbling under the surface. "This is about the diamonds. Stop trying to make it about you. It's business. Yes, I love you, okay? What else do you want?"

Police sirens sounded outside.

He stared at her. "Babe, you didn't, did you?"

"Yes. I have your confession recorded. Now they'll know who the real criminal is."

He took a millisecond to shoot her an evil glare before he turned and sprinted to a back door. Then it slammed shut behind him.

She heard cars stop and the roller door opened.

"Hands behind your head!" someone yelled.

She did as directed and put her hands behind her

head as four officers pointed guns at her. Jack raced to them.

"You're after Ryan Castle, not this woman."

"He ran out the back!" Gretel said.

They lowered their weapons and hurried off, while Jack rushed to her. "Are you all right?"

"I am."

"They surrounded the building. Don't worry, he won't get away."

He went to put his arm around her shoulders and stopped himself. "Sit in the car. I'll be there in a minute." She took the car keys he gave her before he rushed off.

She walked to the car hoping they'd capture him. Minutes later, from inside the car, she watched as two officers escorted a handcuffed Ryan Castle to a police car. It was the best thing she'd ever seen.

Jack slid into the front seat beside her. "We got him."

"Good."

"You sure you're okay?"

"Yes, I just want to go home."

He started the car and Gretel was glad to get away from the place. "I'll get you home after you make a full report."

"Okay," she said in a small voice. "Did you get my phone call? How did you know where I was?"

"I have a tracker in your phone. Just as well you

called me or I would've thought you were in on it with him, or not fully committed."

"I am committed. He called and wanted to meet me. I was going to call you then, but … I'm not sure why I didn't."

Jack said, "He's told us he doesn't know anything about the diamonds. It seems he's going to stick with his original story. I think we'll be able to get him to talk once he's interviewed. I'm not going to let up until I get the truth."

"He deserves to be behind bars after all that he's done."

"I know. Sounds like he's a narcissist for sure." They pulled up at a red light and he stared at her. "Do you normally go for that kind of man?"

Why was he asking? That was what she wanted to know. "Not usually. He wasn't like that at the start." When Jack looked away, a tear trickled down her cheek and she wiped it away with the back of her hand. In her life she'd had everything a girl could dream of, so why had love always eluded her?

JACK BROUGHT Gretel to the police station where she waited alone in an interview room. Ten minutes later, an officer came in with a sandwich and a cup of coffee for her.

She ate the sandwich, which was some kind of

indistinguishable meat with pickles, and then drank the coffee. Neither were very good, but she was hungry enough not to care.

After an hour that Gretel spent dreaming up all the horrible things she wanted to happen to Ryan Castle, Jack Fletcher finally walked in. She looked up at him. "What's going on?"

He sat down opposite her. "He still says he never had the diamonds. He claims he only said those things to you because that's what you wanted to hear and he was trying to get back with you."

"Great. Can't anyone see that he's a pathological liar?" Now she knew he was going to be a free man. She drained the last of her coffee, which was now stone cold. "What's going to happen to him?"

"We've arrested him for obstruction of justice. His lawyer will get him out of that, no doubt. Without more proof of a crime, our hands are tied. He did give you up at the start, so that's going to work in his favor by showing his intentions."

"Proof? I'm telling you he took all the diamonds. I was thrown into prison with no bail and you're telling me he's going to walk free? Walk free with the stolen diamonds?"

"He might."

"What about how he tried to run me down in the street? You've got footage of that."

"That would involve you, put the spotlight on you. We're trying to keep you out of the spotlight."

"Where's the justice in the world? I'll tell you, there is NONE!" She bounded to her feet and paced up and down. "I was arrested, because of him."

"Yes, but you had all the past crimes, which is why you were denied bail. Ryan Castle has done nothing that we can pin on him without involving you any further."

Gretel's mind was racing so fast she wasn't really listening to Jack. "What about the diamond heist we pulled?" She really did the crime. All Ryan did was sit in the car waiting for her.

"He got off that when he gave you up."

Grrrr. She gritted her teeth and regretted asking Ryan about the loot from the Welch house. If he had been involved, now he'd make sure his tracks were better covered.

"Hey, you're not getting off too bad considering all you've done. If you weren't helping us, you'd be back in prison right now."

She was so mad at this moment, she wouldn't mind being back in jail if that meant that Ryan Castle also suffered.

"We'll put a tail on him and hopefully he'll eventually lead us to the diamonds. Now, they'll need your statement about today's events."

"Is there really any point?"

"For the record."

He took her to an interview room where she sat and recounted all the details that she remembered.

JACK HAD WAITED for her to finish and then offered to drive her home.

From the driver's seat Jack turned to look at her. "Will you be okay?"

"Yes. No. Not really. I'm trying to wrap my head around it all."

He stopped the car right outside her building. "I know how you feel. Justice often doesn't get served the way I'd like it either, but as I said, you've just been handed a golden ticket, so I wouldn't be feeling too down."

"I know. And I've got you to thank for that. It will be official soon, right?"

He smiled. "We're working on it. It's as good as official. Stop worrying."

It was easy for him to say.

She opened the door and was about to step out when he said, "Tomorrow, we're focused back on the Glen Welch case."

"Okay." She got out of the car and walked into her building. She hadn't known this working with the FBI was going to be an everyday thing. Two or three times a year was what she'd envisioned. Never had she worked this hard.

When Gretel got into her apartment, she pulled out one of her several disposable cell phones and called Kent and proceeded to tell him all that had just happened.

"You've got to put that creep out of your mind," Kent told her. "It doesn't matter if he walks free and still has the diamonds. You're out of jail. Your freedom is more important than a few lousy diamonds, don't you think?"

"I know. I know you're right, but it bugs me. He's outwitted and outsmarted the FBI and me. He's so smug."

"He hasn't outsmarted anyone. He's just lied his way out of everything. You loved him and he threw it in your face. Walk away and take it as a lesson learned. Education is expensive, whichever way we get it."

"Yeah, I'll never trust again. I've certainly learned that lesson the hard way."

"Just fall in love with someone worthy next time, okay?"

"Okay, wise one." She found it hard to believe Kent, a computer nerd, who rarely left his apartment, was giving her good advice.

Kent chuckled. "Now, want to know what I've learned about the Welch family?"

CHAPTER 26

GRETEL HAD SPENT the last ten minutes complaining about Ryan when all the while Kent had information about the Welch family. "Of course I want to know about it. I hope it's something I don't already know."

"You know they were in debt?" Kent asked.

"Yes. I knew that."

"It's not about the Welch family so much but Ryan and Gizelle. They were close."

"That's interesting."

"They shared the same father, different mothers, and Ryan is quite a bit older. I happened across her phone records and she and Ryan talk at least once a day, sometimes three times a day. What's interesting is the day of Glen Welch's death there were no phone calls between them."

"Because they were together that day and that night

when they were killing him and emptying the safe. Wow. But it's not something that we can prove and Jack keeps carrying on about needing proof. Ryan was in hospital at night and gone the next day. He was so bad he would've needed medical attention or at least someone to help him. Gizelle had to be the one to help him out of the hospital before they killed Glen, stole the jewelry and set up the crime scene."

"Ryan needed Gizelle's help to get to the jewelry, she needed his help to get rid of the stepfather. Everybody wins. Every player wins a prize," Kent said.

"Except me who got the short straw, in life and in love. I can't wait to tell Jack about this. It's something to work with, something we can build on."

"Wait. How are you going to tell him exactly? You can't tell him about me."

"He can subpoena their phone records if he hasn't done so already. I'll give him a hint what to look for. Thanks for finding that out."

"All in a day's work."

"You're nothing short of a genius, Kent."

"I have been called that in the past. I try my best."

She ended the call, changed phones and called Jack. Now she had that news, and she didn't want to wait until morning to see Jack again. He'd be delighted with the valuable information.

"Gretel, how can I help you?"

"I have some interesting information."

"And what's that?"

"Can we talk?"

"Sure. I'm available to talk."

"No, I mean face-to-face."

"I'm just in the office doing paperwork. Do you want me to come and see you?"

"That's okay, I'll come there."

Half an hour later, she was in his office.

Jack Fletcher looked up from his desk and placed his pen down. "What is it that you have to tell me that couldn't wait until tomorrow?"

"It's not something to tell you as such. It's an idea I've had. I was … in a deep meditative state when I was thinking about the relationship Gizelle might have had to her older half-brother. What if they were in it together? She gets rid of her stepfather who she never liked, she and her mother get the insurance money, and Ryan's pay-off for pulling the trigger is the jewelry."

"What am I always telling you about proof?"

"I knew you'd say that. I thought you might find something in their phone records. Do you have them?"

"I can get them quick enough. Just a moment." He tapped some keys on his computer keyboard. "Subpoena underway. Unfortunately, it's not a quick process."

"Good. I'll go home then."

"That was a quick visit."

She flashed him a smile as she walked out wondering how deep Gizelle's involvement was. Could she be wrong about her? Even though she didn't like

Gizelle and never had, was she capable of murder? It was clear she was a liar since she'd told huge lies about the Cleopatra bracelet.

If she got the truth out of Gizelle about that bracelet, she'd be closer to knowing what happened on the night that Glen Welch was killed.

As soon as she was on the sidewalk, she called Kent to get Gizelle's address.

AN HOUR LATER, Gretel was driving slowly past Gizelle's house in the suburbs. It was a low set house with a double garage attached, much the same as every house on the street. No cars sat in the driveway and there was no sign of life. As she drove to the end of the cul-de-sac to do another drive-by, she saw the garage had a window. If she peeped in, she'd know if anyone was home. If Gizelle wasn't there, a search of her house might prove far more fruitful than a conversation with her.

She parked her car a few houses up and walked back to the side of Gizelle's house. When she looked in the window, she was surprised to see Ryan's car. It was the same black car that had almost run her down.

Footsteps sounded behind her. Before she had a chance to turn around, something struck her head.

All went black.

CHAPTER 27

WHEN GRETEL OPENED HER EYES, she winced with pain. She could smell blood and knew it was coming from the back of her head. When she tried to touch the part of her head that hurt, she couldn't. Looking down, she saw why. Ropes wound around her body had her tied to a chair. She tried to move to free herself, but she couldn't.

"Help." Her voice was croaky and not loud at all. After taking a deep breath and summoning all her strength she tried again. "Help!"

Ryan walked in and pointed a gun at her. "Shut up!"

"What are you doing?"

He stepped forward and pointed the gun at her head. "What did you tell them about me?"

"I told them you'd be here at Gizelle's and they're coming to get you." Her words were spat out with venom.

"Why aren't they here already? You've been out cold all night and no one's come to save you. If you knew I was here, you wouldn't have been snooping around. Answer the question."

"I didn't tell them anything. How could I? I know nothing about you."

He crouched down in front of her. "Why are you here?"

"I came to see Gizelle. Find out how she was coping with her stepfather's death, and to offer my condolences."

"How do you know Gizelle?"

"You already know, and I know how you know her too." She was so angry all she wanted was the truth. "Why did you kill Glen Welch?"

"I'll tell you because I know you're not wearing a wire." He sniggered. "I checked already. I was always going to kill Welch one day. I worked out a long time ago that he killed my father. He wanted the one thing my father had that he didn't, my stepmother."

"So, Glen Welch killed your father so he could marry Josephine? You're trying to tell me Glen hadn't heard of divorce? He was a lawyer for Pete's sake."

"One of the men on the boat told me what really happened that night. He saw it with his own eyes and then had to pretend he was asleep. He was plagued with guilt for keeping quiet about it. He sought me out months ago to tell me. Absolve his conscience. It confirmed what I'd thought all along."

That added up with the boat story she'd read about from the files and from the news articles. "What have you done with the Welch jewels and my diamonds?"

"Same old Gretel, only care about yourself. You couldn't care less that my father was killed, could you?"

"I didn't know him. You and I are not friends. I don't care about your life."

Anger hardened his chiseled features. "The diamonds are safe. Now you can tell me where to offload them."

"No. Figure it out for yourself. It's really not that hard. Ask around." He put the gun to her head and she closed her eyes tightly. She heard something click. Nothing. She was still alive. She quickly opened her eyes. "Jackson Forsitto," rolled off her tongue.

"Really?"

"Yes." She hated that she was so weak, but she did want to stay alive.

"Hardly seems he'd need the money."

"That's his cover."

"I'll be back and if I find out you're lying, I'm going to kill you."

"You'll need to give him the password, though."

"What's the password?"

"Pink giraffes fly with umbrellas."

He repeated it and pulled out his phone and wrote it in his notes. Then he looked up at her and lowered his face until it was an inch away from hers. "I'm coming straight back."

"I'm not going anywhere. Obviously. Don't forget my share."

"You won't need it now that you're working with the cops."

"FBI."

He threw his head back and laughed. Her life wasn't supposed to turn out like this, wasn't supposed to end like this. She knew she was going to die. Still strapped to the chair, he dragged her out of the garage and into the house, and then he smirked at her. "Don't go anywhere."

He slammed the door closed behind him. A few seconds later, she heard the garage door go up and his car start.

Her revenge had been giving him that ridiculous password. She couldn't believe he swallowed it. Jackson would know something was amiss. Wriggling her legs about she knew she wasn't going anywhere, but she could move the chair along the floor by shuffling her feet. That wasn't going to help. Not with all the doors in the garage shut and her hands behind her back.

It was a one-hour drive to where Jackson had his retail jewelry store, so that gave her two hours to get out of there. There was no way Jackson would deal with someone who hadn't been given a recommendation.

From within the garage, her cell phone rang. Her bag was in there but how was she going to get it?

Just as she was thinking what to do, she heard a car. He was back.

She froze in fear. He'd kill her for sure. He must've figured out that pink umbrella thing would've backfired for him. She couldn't believe he didn't question her about that. Maybe he was still suffering the after effects of the gunshot wound.

The door flung open and she saw Gizelle. From her face, she knew Gizelle wasn't on her side.

"If it isn't miss fancy pants no good thief." She was holding a small suitcase which she placed down on the floor.

"Hi." Putting the pieces together, she'd been knocked out and now it was the next day. Surely, Jack would be looking for her.

"Ryan told me we had a guest."

"You know that's not his real name, don't you? I mean Ryan is, but Castle isn't. I know that now."

Gizelle crouched down in front of her. "I know more about him than you do. Who do you think told him about you?"

Gretel did her best to hide her surprise.

Gizelle continued, "Hazel told me about you years ago and what you did for a crust."

"Hazel would never—"

"Don't forget she's been a pretty good friend over the years. At the time, she was upset about some

239

boyfriend or other that she'd broken up with and I was comforting her, giving her more and more to drink. We were both drowning our sorrows."

"My sister doesn't drink."

"She was drinking that day. Then you called in the middle of it. You were in Rome at a casino and guess who was also in Rome, and lucky for us he wasn't far from the casino. I had you two meet. It was all my doing." She cackled.

Gretel swallowed hard thinking back to the first time she laid eyes on Ryan Castle. He was handsome, that was what attracted her at the beginning, and then she saw he was getting friendly with one of the big players. A gut feeling had told her he was pulling a sting, but he never approached her. The opposite was the fact, but they did make eye contact and he smiled at her. When the big player next to him didn't look happy, they had words, then Ryan moved to another gambling table and she sat next to him. If she hadn't made that move, they'd never have met. "No. I don't believe you're telling the truth."

"He's a con artist. I was always telling him he could do more and go after bigger things. Mind you, that wasn't the first time your sister mentioned you and what you were doing. At first I found it hard to believe with you being a minister's daughter. I guess you rebelled." She flung a hand in the air. "Whatever."

How could her sister betray her like that? She wasn't even a close friend with Gizelle, as far as what

Hazel had told her. "Can you release me? I'll not say anything to anyone about Ryan tying me up, or anything."

"No. Not until Ryan and I have got to the next stage."

Gretel closed her eyes but then her head swam too much. Fixing her eyes on Gizelle, she asked, "Are you going to kill me?"

"I'm not going to do anything. You were never here. I never saw you."

"What happened to your stepfather?"

"I hated him. He couldn't care less about me. He left Ryan fatherless and when Ryan's mother died a year after his father was killed, he refused to take Ryan in. It was as though he never existed. He paid for boarding school only because Josephine had once been Ryan's stepmother. He didn't even have him home for the holidays."

"That's so awful. He was permanently at boarding school?"

"Yes."

"How did you two get so close?"

"Only as adults."

"How did your mother feel about it?"

Gizelle's face contorted, but at least she was talking. "She had no say in anything. It was my stepfather that was running the show."

"So you killed him?"

"It was the only way. There was no money left. How

would Mom and I survive? The creditors were about to move in on the debts and take the firm and that meant the house would go too. We all knew the crash was coming any day. It was only a matter of time. Now Mom's got his life insurance and the insurance from the jewelry."

"And Ryan's got the jewelry and he's trying to sell it."

A smile spread across her face. "Yes."

"This is unbelievable." Gretel was more annoyed than ever and wanted to bust free but she was strapped tight.

"It had to be done."

"Does your mother know about what you and Ryan did?"

"What *Ryan* did you mean? She knows nothing. She wasn't upset that Glen died, though, I can tell you that much."

"That's a bit sad."

"No one will miss him. My mother didn't really like him, not that much."

"I need to go to the bathroom. Can you untie me?"

"No. Stay there!" Gizelle got to her feet and walked away.

"Gizelle, I really need to go. Ryan's got my car keys somewhere, so I can't leave if that's what you're worried about."

Gizelle then yelled from somewhere within the

house, "And, in case you were wondering, Ryan never loved you. He'd call me and we'd laugh about you."

As hurtful as that was, there was no time to process the comment.

Time was running out. Ryan had killed his step-mother's second husband in cold blood and now he'd be coming back for her, enraged and embarrassed because Jackson Forsitto would've rejected him.

She looked around. In the hallway there was nothing that would cut through the ropes. There were glass sections in the front door and maybe a glass shard could saw through the rope, but Gizelle would hear glass breaking.

She could try pleading with Gizelle again, but Gizelle would have too much to lose since she was in on it with Ryan.

The only thing Gretel could do was scoot along the floor as quietly as she could. The first doorway led to a bedroom. She moved from polished wood to carpeted floor. Bad idea. The carpet was almost impossible to move on. Then on the bedside table, she spotted a cigarette lighter. No. She'd most likely set herself on fire and nobody would be there to put out the flames.

Sitting there alone, roped to a chair, she knew she was done for. The only thing left to do was pray for a miracle, but she wouldn't. She couldn't. Not after everything she'd done.

Then she heard brakes screeching just outside the

garage door. A door slammed. It was Ryan and he was back.

She shut her eyes tightly. "Let it be quick."

Suddenly, she heard the internal door that led into the house flung open. Ryan stood there, enraged, in the bedroom doorway. The tension in the air was thick, the anger thicker.

"Think you're clever, don't you?"

"Why, what happened?"

"He laughed at me."

She was too scared to see the humor. "Did you say the right thing?"

"When I repeated it, he had me thrown out." Slowly, he pulled a gun out of his pocket.

"You can't kill me here. It'll make a mess on the carpet."

"I'm doing it Dexter style. I'm wrapping you in plastic." He dragged her into the kitchen. "Gizelle, I need plastic. We'll have to kill her."

Gizelle ran to them. "But don't you need her?"

"No. Get the plastic"

Gizelle went to the pantry and produced a roll of plastic.

"I'll need more than that."

"That's all I've got."

He set the gun down, and from his pocket produced black gloves and pulled them on his hands. Then he started the first wrap of plastic around her midsection while Gizelle watched, her mind churning.

"Wait. You're doing it wrong," Gretel told him. "Dexter wrapped the room in plastic."

"It'll work."

"No, stop. Let me go and I won't say anything. No one knows what you've done. They've got no idea. They're totally clueless."

He then wrapped a sheet of plastic across her mouth. "I've been wanting to do that for a long time."

"I've got money! I'll pay you to let me go." Her words came out muffled because of the tightness of the plastic. The more she talked the less air she had. She poked out her tongue trying her best to make a hole in the plastic.

There were only minutes left to live. She tried to scoot herself along the floor to get away, but heavy hands held her. More plastic was wrapped around her torso.

Were they going to shoot her in the head and through the heart?

There was no way out. She hated that the last sounds she would hear were Ryan's breaths and the last smells would be the aftershave that she once loved.

She couldn't breathe, and pain filled her lungs as they begged for air. Everything was fading. In the distance, she heard a siren. Was it a police car? It sounded like one. Maybe she was dreaming as she died.

There was no time for regrets or what ifs.

Darkness.

CHAPTER 28

GRETEL'S whole body spasmed with pain. Somewhere in her consciousness floated the idea she'd been shot. Air. She could breathe. She opened her eyes and saw figures moving around. It was too much work to keep watching. Her eyelids closed again.

"Talk to me, Gretel. Are you all right?"

It was Jack's voice!

But was she dreaming?

She tried to speak, but it wouldn't come.

"Say something. Are you okay?"

With difficulty, she breathed out, "Yes."

Her eyes opened and she saw Jack. The next moment, her mind was clearer and … she was stretched out on the floor and Jack was sitting, cradling her upper body in his arms. "Stay still. The paramedics are on their way."

She struggled to sit up. When she looked around, there was no sign of either of her captors. "What …"

"Ryan and Gizelle have both been arrested. Don't worry about that now. Just get your strength back."

"Has the jewelry been found?"

"We found the Welch jewelry in his car. He'll be going away for a long time."

That was the best news she'd ever heard. "She said Ryan killed Glen."

"Who said that?"

"Gizelle, I'm also certain she was the one who helped Ryan out of the hospital that night of the murder."

The paramedics arrived and Jack walked out of the room and left her with them. After examining her they told her it was a good thing Jack had done CPR. She'd gone into heart failure after Ryan had stopped her breathing, and Jack had saved her life. Even after hearing that, she refused to go to the hospital. Her ribs were pretty sore from the CPR chest compressions, but when the paramedics poked and prodded them it didn't feel like any were cracked.

"I'll go home and rest. I'll be okay. I'm breathing."

"I'll make sure she's okay."

She looked up to see that Jack was back in the room. "I really want to go home."

"I'll drive you. Someone can come get your car tomorrow."

He helped her to his car. All strength had drained from her body, but she was grateful to be alive.

As they drove, the events played out in her mind like the living real-life nightmare that it was. "How did it all play out just now?"

"We got a call from a reputable jeweler. He was pretty certain a man who'd just come in had some stolen jewelry. He recognized one of the pieces as coming from the Welch collection."

Jackson Forsitto had done a good job. He'd saved her life. "That was a lucky break."

"It was. Then we had the highway patrol stop him, and a quick look at his GPS told us where he'd been. That led us to you." He glanced over at her. "Do you have someone who can stay with you tonight?"

"I do but I'd rather be alone." Normally she would've called her sister, but she was majorly upset with her. Hazel had broken the golden rule of silence about what Gretel did for a living. Now, she was truly alone. Trusting people only led to disappointment. "Thanks for saving my life."

He glanced over at her. "I just did what anyone would do."

"Thanks for caring. I know you could be questioning Gizelle and Ryan right now and instead you're taking me home."

He grinned. "It won't hurt to let them stew for a while. They can wait."

When they arrived at her place, he insisted on

coming in and making sure she was okay. He sat her down on the couch. "I'll get you something to eat."

"There's nothing here. I normally eat out or order in. You know, shop by the day."

"How about I order us some Chinese?" He plumped up the cushions behind her.

"Sounds perfect," she said only to be polite.

"I'm pleased you're hungry. That's a good sign." He picked up his phone and called in an order. Then he walked into her bedroom and came back with a blanket and spread it over her. "I'll make you some of that herbal tea while we're waiting for the food."

After they ate, Jack stayed with her until late. She must've dozed off after their meal because she heard the click of the front door as he quietly let himself out. It felt good that someone had been there for her.

The next morning Gretel woke from the sun streaming through the windows in the living room. She couldn't wait to find out how the case had progressed overnight. But first things first. She tried to sit up but every muscle in her body ached. When she finally moved the blanket off her, all she wanted was heat on her body and then she'd take something strong for the pain.. After that, she'd call Jack.

Hot water had never felt so good. Closing her eyes she turned the shower on full and let it wash over her head and down her back. Mentally, she washed away all traces of Ryan Castle and the awful things he'd done to her.

She stepped out of the shower and reached for a white fluffy towel, trying the best she could to cope with the aches. Not only was she in pain, but it also hurt to breathe. She wrapped one about her body and towel-dried her hair with the other. With no energy to blow-dry her hair and style it as usual, she gave it a quick dry and then ran her hands through it. When she switched off the hairdryer, she heard a knock on the door.

Gretel froze. She hoped it was Jack. Forgetting she was in a towel, she hobbled to the door and saw from the monitor it was Jack. Then she looked down at herself. "Hold on a minute." Sore all over, she carefully walked to her dressing room, and pulled on the first thing she saw, t-shirt and jeans. Now she was in a good mood—he'd have news of Ryan's charges. Momentarily forgetting her pain, she opened the door smiling, and then she saw his glum face. "What is it?"

"Bagels." He held up a bag. "And coffee." He held a cardboard tray with two coffees in the other hand.

"Come in."

He walked further into the apartment and then turned around to face her. "I have bad news."

"Wait. Let me sit." Rather than sit on the couch, she sat on the stool at the countertop so she wouldn't have to bend.

He sat on the stool beside her and pushed the coffee along to her. "This is yours. We don't have him."

She stared at him trying to work out what he said. "What do you mean?"

"We had him in custody—"

Now she was sick to the stomach. She knew the 'him' was Ryan Castle. They'd caught him red-handed trying to kill her and with the stolen goods in his car. "You don't have Ryan?"

"He got bail this morning."

"Bail? Are you kidding me?"

"I'm not. From the court, he was forced into a white SUV much like the ones we saw at the lake house."

"This can't be happening." She took a mouthful of coffee. "After all this."

He ripped open the bagel package and handed her one.

"Thanks."

"Gizelle told us everything. Ryan forced her to give him the combination by threatening her and her mother's safety. He also killed Glen Welch."

She looked across at him. "Did she get bail too?"

"Yes."

"They both tried to kill me. Ryan, twice in the last few days. First with the car and then …" She stared into the dark liquid she had cupped in her hands. They were both liars. What really happened was anyone's guess. There was so much she hadn't told Jack and now she felt bad because he'd saved her life and seemed so nice.

"Don't worry, Gretel, they'll both get time. I'll see to it. I can promise you that."

"That makes me feel better." She took a bite of bagel. When she thought back to the interior base on the safe that she'd left undone, it still hit her as odd that it hadn't been seen and reported by Josephine as yet. Unless she really had thought the police had left it like that. And, who was that man who'd tried to stop her at the Welches' house? She was positive it was the man she'd seen at the funeral.

"Are you okay?"

She looked into his concerned eyes. "I'm fine." She set her bagel down and took another sip of coffee. When she finished swallowing, she said, "We still don't know who those men were that were shooting at us at Ryan's lake house." She gulped. "Wait. Do you think those men kidnapped him, or something? You mentioned the SUV."

"That's what I was saying. He certainly didn't look like he went with them willingly."

"You saw it?"

"Yes. I've just come from there."

"Hmm. I wonder if they've got him because they know he's got my diamonds ... I mean the stolen diamonds. You have the Welch jewelry in evidence and they can't get any of that."

"Correct. He can't stay underground forever. He's been ordered to report every two days. If he misses that day, we put out a warrant for him and he goes to jail until his trial."

"They should never have let him out."

"First offender."

"First offender with a fake identity. He's tried to kill me three times now. Unbelievable."

"I know. I was surprised he got bail. I think you're safe from him. He's got bigger things to worry about, if those people who grabbed him don't kill him first. I'm sorry that helping me put you in so much danger."

She swallowed hard, not wanting to jeopardize her deal. "I'm involved either way. I won't rest until he's behind bars." In her heart, she knew if Ryan got away from those men, he'd disappear and he'd never stand trial. "I won't rest until he's behind bars and it's proven that he took those diamonds." The dark recesses of her mind were working overtime. The best outcome would be if she got the diamonds back and made it look like the men in the white SUVs took them, that would be a plan—a very good plan. Even, a perfect plan.

"Are you okay, Gretel?"

She looked into his handsome face and smiled as happiness whirled around her. Sitting there with him made her feel appreciated. Someone cared about her. "I'm fine."

"We appreciate all the help you've been, Gretel. I'm recommending that they push your paperwork ahead."

"Really? Did my lawyer contact you?"

"Yes."

"Thanks. I truly appreciate it. I just feel like there are so many loose ends. We still don't know if The Shadows, the gang who stole from people who'd stolen, was real or imagined."

"Yes, there are criminals who do that kind of thing. Is there an organized gang called The Shadows? Highly unlikely. Who were those men in the SUVs? Ryan crossed you, so I'm thinking they were the result of a person he crossed some time before he met you. They were looking for Ryan and for all we know they might've thought that I was Ryan. We have a similar height and similar build."

"You look nothing alike."

"Yes, but from a distance they could've easily mistaken me for him."

"I guess that's true."

"What else are you bothered about?"

"Nothing." She was bothered about a whole lot of things, but nothing she wanted to share with him. Monica was against her. Had she sent someone to spy on her, guessing she'd go back to the Welch house that night?

"You've done a good job for us, Gretel."

"I have? I can't help feeling I haven't done much."

He chuckled. "You flushed out Ryan Castle and because of you we've arrested Ryan Castle and Gizelle. Both of them killed Glen Welch, we know that now. It'll be interesting to see if the jury believes Gizelle about it all being Ryan's doing."

"That will be good to watch—someone doing to him what he did to me."

"Life comes full circle very often. Karma, if you believe in all that."

"I hope he doesn't leave the country."

"He can try, but he won't get very far." He took a mouthful of coffee. "Stop looking so worried. We have to shelve the Welch case until the trial. I won't let Ryan get away. I've told you that. Time to move onto our next job."

She looked into his eyes. "I'm looking forward to it." He was so handsome, so caring, so kind, and he believed in her. He deserved someone so much better than Monica. Someone … someone like her … perhaps?

THE NEXT BOOK IN THE SERIES

The next book in the Gretel Koch Jewel Thief series is:
Book 2 Controlled

Gretel Koch is doing her best to curb her stealing
ways,
but when the Purple Promise, a rare 22 carat purple
diamond, is on display offered for sale to the highest
bidder, the temptation is almost greater than she can
bear.
What will she do when her old life collides with
her new?

Thank you for reading Shiny Things.
I hope you enjoyed it. To stay up to date with my new releases and special offers, add your email at my website in the newsletter section.
https://samanthapriceauthor.com/

Blessings,
Samantha Price

ABOUT SAMANTHA PRICE

USA Today Bestselling author, Samantha Price, wrote stories from a young age, but it wasn't until later in life that she took up writing full time. Formally an artist, she exchanged her paintbrush for the computer and, many best-selling book series later, has never looked back.

Samantha is happiest on her computer lost in the world of her characters. She is best known for the Ettie Smith Amish Mysteries series and the Expectant Amish Widows series.

www.SamanthaPriceAuthor.com

Samantha loves to hear from her readers. Connect with her at:

samantha@samanthapriceauthor.com
www.facebook.com/SamanthaPriceAuthor
Follow Samantha Price on BookBub
Twitter @ AmishRomance
Instagram - SamanthaPriceAuthor

CPSIA information can be obtained
at www.ICGtesting.com
Printed in the USA
LVHW040212291019
635549LV00003B/787

9 781700 128553